THIRTY-THREE

CROWS

THIRTY-THREE CROWS

CROWS

A NOVEL

ROGER R. ZIEGLER

ISBN-13: 978-0-578-96903-9

Cover design by: Scott Bowlin
Printed in the United States of America

DEDICATION PAGE

Dedicated to our dearly loved son, Noah. How I had hoped you were here to partake in the joy of sharing this story with the world, as I wrote line after line and chapter by chapter. Not a day goes by without me thinking of you. I miss your everything. Rest in paradise.

TABLE OF CONTENTS

CHAPTER 1

Her tears were released without warning. They departed suddenly as if they were staged; drops of ache ready and waiting for moments when they would be summoned. They crept down slowly forging a trail directly beneath the inner points of her eyes. Downward they crawled until they gathered at the corners of her mouth, as Samantha's chin trembled. Grief led her through the several days that followed the passing of her dearest husband, Russell. It was necessary and she allowed it.

Her swollen eyes studied each detail of his face through swells of new-fallen teardrops. Even within the dimness of the early morning, she could not put down her favorite black and white photograph of Russell. It was a treasure that had immense value; an 8x10 portrait taken of him during their honeymoon was sealed in a mahogany wood picture frame. The ornate border design complemented the contours of his chiseled features perfectly. It did not matter that she was not able to visibly enjoy the photograph as she sat in the unlit space. No, because the hundreds of hours she already spent staring into his eyes before burned into memory.

Her fingers gently swept across the glass as she outlined the area of his face. It was the closest she would get to mimic when she caressed his cheek like she did so many times before. Samantha imagined his voice calling to her and she considered answering verbally, but she was quickly reminded that he was gone. Constant disappointment afflicted her heart.

If it had not been for her son, Dominic, she would be on a course headed for terminal despair and intense depression. Samantha loved immensely and, as a result, remained somewhat unguarded and vulnerable to emotional ambushes when they pertained to those whom she held close to her heart. She also possessed a strength that flowed from her passion for caring for others. An attribute that fared well in her role as an elementary school teacher.

Her hand retreated from the framed photograph and it reached out beside her to pull back the tall, dense curtain and revealed a spacious living room window. Her view of the morning scene unfolding outside was spectacular and she desperately needed to witness the sunny invitation that was soon to rise for her pleasure. Once the drape was pushed to one side, her eyes detached from her stare fixed upon the framed picture she held and turned to enjoy the view through her window. Both eyes squinted as they received new light from the early day.

Her attention was now set on the splendor of the world outside. Even from her plush leather recliner beside the window, she was captivated by the sheer grandeur of such a wonderful setting. Her street was rather wide and broad; her neighbors were at least a two-acre span away in both directions. The trees that lined her front lawn separated her widespread, green grassy field from the street and her driveway was parallel to a long row of bushes and clusters of sunflowers. Across from her property was a direct view of rolling hills set well beyond the street with no obstruction. Behind the hills was a majestic mountain range that reminded her of distant castle walls, similar to those that provide security. As if they stood guard from danger to the north. Above the tall peaks rose the blistering light of the climbing sun, the deepest bluest skies, and occasional clusters of silver clouds. This was certainly the most beautiful place.

Like many others who lived here, she believed it was the perfect place to reside and call home. It was called Esid Arapym and no other place rivaled its eye-beholding wonder. The land was vast and had numerous regions called by other names spread over a large country, but Esid Arapym still had that community feel with a bustling downtown area. It was a place where many had lived, but because of the sheer span of its borders, it felt rural in most areas.

Her eyes scanned from left to right, over the rolling hills, and fell upon the horizon. For a few moments, she escaped her cozy home and imagined herself soaring over the countryside. Almost like a bird set free to dash through uncharted open spaces reserved for creatures with wings. In the distance, she noticed one flying across the open sky. It had a broad wingspan with long, heavy strokes that propelled its body through the air with ease. She imagined being carried away from grief by the power of its flight. An escape from the painful memory of the loss of her husband.

"I miss you, Russ," her voice cracked with weariness and a heavy tone. "I wish you were here."

Her arms clutched the frame tightly to her chest and she began to sob with heaviness. Samantha fell back into her chair with her head down over the photograph. The light from a fresh day spilled into her moment and slowly illuminated her living room with a soft orange glow. She sat there in silence, steeped in pure sadness. It was all she could do and that was acceptable to her.

Her long dark hair draped both sides of her round face. Normally, her dark eyes conveyed a friendliness about her, but now on this side of her loss, grief was all you could see behind those swollen eyes. They did not hide her pain at all.

She didn't have a family to lean on other than her six-year-old son, Dominic. Her deceased parents were missed for years now and she had no siblings. Russell's parents had also died four years after their marriage. After their passing, his brother had moved away and they never heard from him again. She felt the bondages of isolation with the passing of her husband. Seven years of marriage now abruptly collapsed by death. Her dreams of growing old together and becoming grandparents later in life had now dissolved.

She depended greatly on her friends and especially her closest friend, Dani. The two were so like-minded and she was her maid of honor in Samantha's wedding. If there was one person who could always make her laugh or raise her spirits no matter what was occurring in life, it was Dani. She had an outgoing and spunky personality that made her a fun person to be around. Now, with the current turn of events in her life, Samantha would have to rely on her for a great deal of support.

As the days continued to unfold from the unforgiving scrolls of time, she learned how to grieve and still move forward. Samantha would not allow herself to be stuck or become a hostage to such things as depression. No, she would learn how to rise and pour even more into her son and those around her.

This was a new beginning for her, a strange new chapter. She was not ready for what would come next, but none of us ever are.

~

The fog had suddenly lifted from her majestic garden. The lingering thick mist seeped through a dense wall—a tree line at the outer edge of her property that quietly kept guard—and retreated away from her backyard into the woods. Each night a dense moisture covering kept all foliage nourished. Since there was no rainfall in Esid Arapym, this dewy blanket was vital to the land. Now the grand display of various assorted blossoms and colorful clusters were open to the sunshine's rays.

Samantha thoroughly enjoyed her expansive and manicured grounds. Her backyard garden was her sanctuary and place of peaceful respite during stages of grief. With Russell's passing still a brief six months earlier, so the sense of deep loss was felt like raw skin scraped by the ripest lemons. His passing reminded her of how something as terrible as Stillwhorm Syndrome could destroy so many families.

She held onto Dominic ever so tightly and even more so during the months that followed her husband's death. She cherished every solitary moment and made the full complement of a day's portion of time count. During Samantha's garden getaways Dominic bounced around through rows of bushes and lofty blooms, but he stayed close by. Often with a stick in his hand and a smile on his face, his life was very simple. He loved his mother very much and missed his father deep in his heart.

Russell left Samantha with the means to take care of her and Dominic from their savings account, but mostly from a sizeable insurance policy. When Russell died, she initially took several weeks off from her position at the school where she taught second-grade students. But, she had no desire to return. It became a sort of early retirement for the time being. Now she spent her days with Dominic with trips to the library, in playgroups with other children his age, and healing moments in her garden. Life was purposely simplified and organized in such a way that staved off chaos.

She couldn't help but remain in heavy thought about the loss of her husband. It was shocking and staggering to comprehend. Yet, the chilling reality continued to replay its barrage of agonizing scenery left behind. It was her heart that bled and her suffering that cast its shadow upon her future.

And then, one day it struck her mind like a swift-moving arrow. She realized at some point in her son's life he would probably fall victim to the very same sickness. Stillwhorm Syndrome, the diabolical illness that had ravaged these residents for generations, could take her son's life next. This illness was spread through the bloodlines of families. A cold reminder that pure evil had no favorites or did not keep a list of those lives somehow immune to its taste of poisonous bitterness. Dominic could one day, just like his father, contract the deadly affliction and it suddenly rattled her to no end.

Little did she know this very curse was unleashed for such a time as this; to strike down the potential of good that could rise through this place and specifically through her family. It was patient and methodical. It was a deadly disease inflicted by the hands of wicked intent and abolished hope with the fear of its terminal venom. Once diagnosed, no one was able to escape certain death.

Her son was all she had left that was meaningful and pleasant. Dominic's eyes calmly set her at ease. His smile comforted any uneasy thoughts and uninvited fear. She was the most grateful mother in all of Esid Arapym, because of her one and only son. Because of her sweet boy, Dominic.

Samantha knew what could be done to dissolve this threat. She understood there was a preventative cure and it was the only way to ensure his protection from this sickness that ravaged healthy lives. There was one sure way to keep him from tasting this poison permanently. It was an opportunity that could only be made on someone's thirty-third birthday—that day and no other. And her birthday was closing in fast. She was about to turn thirty-three years of age. It was perfect timing and the only sliver of opportunity for her to save him.

Most people did not believe in this fairy tale passed down from one generation to the next; that a powerful act of sacrifice could grant someone perpetual immunity from any sickness. But Samantha believed it was possible. She recalled her parents teaching her about the ways of this remarkable event and it was as real to her as the threat of Stillwhorm.

This powerful gesture required a decision and an act to enable its sustaining power upon the recipient. In this case, the recipient would be Dominic. The decision was already made in her heart. But it also came with a specific curse attached. One that could not be reversed once it was set in motion. A curse that would befall the grantor; a certain doom would strike in the form of Stillwhorm Syndrome. By this very act, Samantha would trade her life for her son's perfect health. On the surface, it sounded plausible, yet deep down she could sense the trauma he would endure. But, to save him this was his only hope.

~

Several weeks had now passed. A seasonal shift into warmer days meant beaming sunshine would attract those who enjoy outdoor activities. And Samantha loved being outdoors. Sometimes a few coworkers, from the school where she once taught, would enjoy the warm evenings with her. She spent time enjoying the company of her friends as often as she could. Especially with Dani, her best friend.

It was during one evening while they both shared a quiet dinner at their favorite restaurant, Dani asked Samantha a piercing question.

"Sam, do you ever think about Dominic's future? I don't mean his education or starting a family. You know, getting sick one day?"

Her friend's words carried the weight of concern and were not meant to catch Samantha off guard. But they did.

"I try not to dwell on what could happen to him," Samantha's eyes shifted from her plate up to her friend's caring face. "But I get it. More than anyone else, I get it."

She glanced back down to her food and tossed her salad aimlessly with her fork. Then the tears began to escape her eyes.

"Since Russell's passing, I've been thinking a lot about that. Dommie getting this disease. And it terrifies me," said Samantha. "He was recently tested. I'm just waiting for the results."

"Sorry," said Dani. "I didn't mean to bring it up."

She reached out her hand and held Samantha's.

"It's alright," replied Samantha as she wiped her cheeks with her cloth napkin. "It just scares me."

Her friend smiled and reassured her.

"I love you and will always be here. No matter what."

"Thank you," Samantha replied and gently smiled in return. "I only want what's best for him."

They both enjoyed the rest of their evening and spoke about plans to enjoy the countryside soon. They laughed and did not mention anything else about Dominic, Russell, or anything related to sickness. Fear could easily take over and wreck any hope. She had to push back against it. Because the anticipation of such despair causes the living to compromise their quality of life. It can consume their thoughts long before any chance of adversity happening. And that is not living at all.

Two days after their evening together Samantha received an important letter in the mail. It was from the local medical center that specialized in Stillwhorm Syndrome. A place that was far too familiar to her because of Russel's treatment during his final weeks. She stood at her mailbox at the end of her driveway near the road and was paralyzed with fear. *Could this be the results from Dominic's tests?* Her thoughts raced and her anxiety brewed.

She had taken him to the doctor's office for testing and now after two weeks, she was about to learn the outcome. The goal was to determine through specific bloodwork if he would be a victim of the same illness that took his father from them. Because Dominic was Russel's son and the illness traveled mainly through lineage, Samantha decided to have the specific tests administered for confirmation. Not only would it identify the strain typically found in early detection, but the test could also reveal the timeframe of when it could begin to devour the host.

Her hands shook beneath the warm afternoon sunshine as she held the tan envelope. She closed her eyes for a few seconds, then used her index finger to break the seal. After her hand removed the letter and unfolded it she began to quickly read the contents.

Her eyes scanned effortlessly through the first paragraph filled with greetings and empty formalities. As she reached the second paragraph her eyes widened. Her breathing became rapid, shallow, and tense. Fear swelled inside her eyes as she continued to process the results. It was far worse than she had expected. Her face slowly rose from behind the document and she lifted her gaze to the skies.

"No," she whispered and shook her head. "No…no."

As if she misread the information, she plunged her face back to the letter to read it again. But there was no mistaking the bitter news. Dominic tested positive for the strain of Stillwhorm that remained dormant early before it would be triggered to begin its assault on the body. Triggered somehow by unknown factors. He was fine now and as healthy as can be. But the letter continued to inform her that early indications suggested he would certainly fall victim to the disease by age ten to twelve. It was not the typical lifespan of most patients consumed by this sickness; most of the time people in their thirties or forties would begin fighting the outbreak of the disease. On occasion, some people over sixty would begin their bouts.

This news wrecked her deeply. She fooled herself into thinking she would be able to endure hard facts from his testing. But now that this was real and confirmed, it was obvious that she was an emotional mess. She hid the letter in a secret place so that Dominic would not find it. This news was not something she wanted to share with him.

Samantha could not sleep later that night. In the deep darkness of her room, she stared into the chilling thought of losing her sweet boy. She wrestled with it and invited fear into her life. It consumed her mind and unsettled her heart. She tried to tame those overpowering thoughts, but she was helpless against such predators.

She began to whisper a new incantation with resolve.

"I can't let him die. I won't let that happen."

CHAPTER 2

The colorful assortment of birthday invitations made for a tough decision. The friendly store clerk stood by Samantha's side while she held up four options she liked. Both of their eyes scanned each one as they were compared with each other.

Her upcoming unique birthday celebration meant that she could invite anyone she pleased. The attendees, however, felt they could also be a recipient of a wish transfer and not merely guests there to enjoy the festivities. According to traditions, it was customary to invite those who were potential recipients. Either they had been fighting an illness (in most cases it was Stillwhorm) or someone healthy but a possible recipient to prevent any illness in their future.

You could say that Samantha allowed other people's burdens to trickle into the space reserved for her aim to protect her son. She always cared deeply for others and those who knew her understood this best. But Samantha could only see her son's face when she was alone at night. Those moments when she closed her eyes and invite her dreams, her Dommie was right there every time. She could not stand the thought of losing her child. And she made her wish recipient decision long before her search for birthday invitations. It was always Dominic.

She gathered the final two prospects in her hands and held them out one at a time in front of her. Then, with a snappy tone, she confirmed her selection.

"Yup. This is the one."

The employee smiled and she carried the box that contained the ivory and teal invitations with matching envelopes lined with a bright teal foil. They were perfect for the occasion.

She paid for them and thanked the clerk for her help as she turned to leave the store.

"You're welcome, Sam. Have a wonderful birthday party," said the employee.

She waved and smiled in return with a happy voice. Most people in town knew each other and they called Samantha by her nickname. Sam was fitting.

Dominic was only a few shops away spending time with James Clark at his ice cream shop. Mr. Clark owned and operated the business alone, except for a couple of high school kids who handled the duties during the evening hours. He was a grandfather to three children and enjoyed making Dominic's day with a fresh scoop of his favorite bubble gum ice cream. He did not mind watching him while Samantha went to pick out her birthday invites. Not at all.

The door creaked open and the small bell attached to the frame jingled as Samantha walked in to get Dominic.

"Thanks for watching Dommie," she said as her hand reached over the counter with money for his treat.

"No, you keep that, Sam."

Mr. Clark generously replied.

"It's always a pleasure spending a few minutes with my little buddy."

James had the biggest heart and usually gave away free ice cream to the kids here in town. Especially to Dominic.

"How's Mrs. Clark these days?"

Samantha's voice said in a concerned way.

"She's been on my heart lately."

12

"Well, she's a fighter. Her strenuous treatments have taken the wind out of her step, but she seems to have some strength to get around some."

His eyes squinted beneath a heavy frown with the slightest conversation about his wife's struggle with her illness. She began her fight with Stillwhorm six months earlier. He hated the fact that she was stricken with it.

"I'm glad to hear. Please don't hesitate to call me for anything. You have my number."

Samantha answered with grace and a warm smile. She knew exactly how this illness affects families. Her wounds were fresh from losing Russell.

Mr. Clark beamed with his biggest smile in response to her gracious offer.

"Thank you very much. I will. You've been through so much yourself. I'll let Judy know you stopped in today."

Mr. Clark waved goodbye to them both as Dominic hopped down from his chair holding the half-eaten cone in one hand and a crumpled napkin in the other.

"Goodbye, Mr. Clark," Samantha said as she opened the door for her son.

"Bye-bye," said Dominic waving his free hand.

The door caused the bell to ring again and she stepped out into the rest of her day. She appreciated these types of moments with Dominic and did not take any bit of it for granted.

They walked to their car and climbed in. Samantha carefully placed the boxed invitations in the back seat.

"Thanks for waiting patiently. I needed a few minutes to decide on my invites to my birthday party," said Samantha.

"I like his ice cream. It's my favorite."

Dominic's demeanor was always so upbeat.

During their drive home, they talked about adventures in Dominic's make-believe place. He began to tell his mother about this pretend world he made up in his mind shortly after his father died. It was a safe way to cope with such a difficult loss.

His pretend world was filled with wild trees that towered as high above him as skyscrapers and colors in the skies that were found in his mother's breathtaking garden. A place where he imagined amazing birds that spoke to him and helped him find his way through treacherous adventures. Dominic imagined having special powers there and he used them to fight against many terrible things. Yeah, it was obvious to Samantha this place made him very happy.

As they enjoyed the drive in the warmth of the day, she couldn't help but think of Mr. and Mrs. Clark. Her bout with her health must be a huge stress to their home. They were very close to their grown children and their grandkids. It was the time in their lives meant for family and enjoying simple pleasures. Mrs. Clark weighed on her mind heavily, then she glanced toward Dominic who continued describing his latest adventure as he nibbled on the last of his cone. She couldn't think of ever losing him to such a horrible bully this illness had become.

The matter at hand was crystal clear: she would leave behind her beautiful 6-year-old son and he would be raised by someone else. Dominic would not have his mother to love and nurture him through the difficult parts of his life. A staggering thought, but he would have his life to live and that gave her the greatest reassurance.

Samantha was nurtured by parents who both devoted themselves to raise their daughter with a loving lens. She would grow from an innocent child to a loving adult completely armed with compassion for others. The world around her, the people who walked this journey of life alongside her, and anyone outside of herself would be regarded as a precious life. Samantha grew to see others in this powerful light and placed such high value on those who lived in her community.

She formed character traits that sustained belief in men, women, children—everyone, to the point that a stranger was considered a family member, in a sense. She observed life through this lens that focused on every other individual and their needs, and less upon herself. Although she still practiced self-care and possessed a healthy self-image, Samantha was quick to aid others, take on their hurts, and found solitude in giving of herself to those in need.

Her mother and father were very proud of their daughter. They both knew she held the courage to make a difference in this life for lives that desperately required someone to love them. Courageous and willing to be that selfless crusader in a world that craved hope. Yes, she was in a perfect position to become a heroine.

Samantha was committed to her decision to save her son, despite her fate. And nothing or no one would stand in her way. It was a fierce determination that propelled her to this act. There is nothing that compares with the love a mother has for her child.

The will to proceed with the thirty-third birthday wish required utmost respect. This mystery was not accommodating or gentle to those who tested its power. It swept lives with hurricane-force winds and never apologized for its rage. To take hold of this would leave one unguarded on a collision course with a dark death. And death's name was spoken with a violent tongue.

~

The Discovery

Long ago, from generations past, there was a man who lived in solitude among the outer regions. His name was Solomon Childs and he spent the greater part of his life in dedication to discovering a way to help the people of Esid Arapym. Early in his life, he was bludgeoned with grief when tragedy struck his family. His parents became very ill during his late adolescence and, after a short and tumultuous year of watching them helplessly succumb to a disease, they both passed away within hours of each other.

Before his death, Solomon's father challenged him, his only child, to take these experiences and use them to help humanity. The young man agreed, and he was bequeathed with his parent's family fortune and wealthy estate to support his life's pursuit. He mourned deeply at his father and mother's passing; that became the catalyst for Solomon's depression, and he became stunted emotionally. His seclusion in the estate was his fortress, but he remained focused in pursuit of helping others. Perhaps he could find a way to prevent or cure the devastation caused by the sickness that took his parents from him.

Deeply devoted to his calling, he studied hundreds of volumes from his father's prized library. They included reference books, documented studies, and other published journals about a broad scope of biological studies. Medical practices and other forms of science and discovery were tediously researched. His findings only brought him to frustration after years of intense reading, studying, and close observations of these brilliant recordings.

In between lengthy research sessions, he would take long walks throughout his property and marvel at the striking beauty the countryside offered. He could walk in any direction for miles and not reach the limits of the grounds. The Childs' Estate was vast and spanned over much territory.

Thirty-three Crows

Far off in the distance, to the north, his eyes spotted the tree his father spoke of. He recalled the moment he was warned about its fruit and to never eat it. As a child, Solomon asked his father why he could not taste it. His father sternly counseled his son and explained it would make him very sick.

"Is it sweet?" the curious boy asked.

"No," answered his father in a firm tone, "Its bitterness will sour your stomach and make you ill. We don't eat this fruit in our home." As a result, the boy never disobeyed and never ate it.

But that didn't prevent the boy from wandering off across the rolling hills near the ominous tree referred to as Mara by his father. From a safe but short distance, young Solomon would curiously examine its massive branches, a huge canopy of clusters with leaves larger than normal, and the bright purple and yellow colored fruit hanging plentifully from within. The sound of many crows could be heard from a long distance. Their enormous gathering nearly drowned out the overwhelming size and proud display of Mara. Mysteriously, the flock of birds remained on this particular tree only. There were countless other trees as far as the eye could see, but these crows chose Mara as if they stood guard over something precious. He remembered the eerie birds locked in cold stares directed towards him as they cawed and barked with a shriek, ear-piercing tone. It was unsettling. If they were protecting this tree somehow, he wanted nothing to do with them.

On one cloudy day, Solomon hovered over his desk studying one of the library's references concerning rare horticulture. As he turned one of the pages, his discovery was certain. A tree that closely resembled the great one he remembered as a child was pictured in front of him. It was positively and unmistakably

Mara. The fruit colors, the massive size—everything was a match. He smiled as if he stumbled upon something significant.

It was at that precise moment that his concentration was interrupted by an irritating noise. The sound was familiar and startled him. *Caw, caw!* It was a crow frantically shrieking from outside of the window by the study. He looked up and angrily told the menace to fly away. The bird continued to annoy him. He waved his hand to scare the bird, but it remained and it was unaffected by his attempt.

He stood abruptly and shouted at the crow to leave.

"Go away!"

But it only became more agitated and louder.

"This persistent pest is annoying," he mumbled to himself.

Solomon hurried outside to scare him off and he was unexpectedly met by a swarm of noisy crows perched on his car parked in the driveway. There were at least a couple dozen of them, rowdy and agitated. It caught him by surprise to see such an enormous gang of birds that seemed ready to attack but didn't. He rushed to the driver's side of his vehicle with his arms flailing as he shouted at them. The group of feathered pests retreated in flight, like they rehearsed this scenario, and then suddenly landed on a wood fence about a stone's throw away. He stared now with a bit of hatred as it seemed they were mocking him with their behavior.

Slowly and methodically, the crows began to fly a few at a time closer to his car and land just about fifteen feet away on the road directly in front of him. They taunted with their cries and were frantic in their actions. *That's it*, he thought, *I'll just drive them off with my car.* So, he quickly climbed in behind the wheel and started the engine. He set the car in motion and burst forward at them aggressively, but they suddenly flew upwards to avoid being struck. He stopped the car quickly by stomping on the brakes. The tires froze and skidded across dirt and gravel. Through the settling dust, he could see them forming all over again on the road not far in front of him. *This is a game*, he thought. He sped off again towards them and the crows once again fled from his pursuit. This happened over and over until he realized they might be trying to lead him somewhere. As odd as this game of cat and mouse had appeared perhaps he would soon find out what they were trying to communicate.

After driving through the open countryside of their estate, he was now following the flock of crows in flight toward the direction of Mara, the tree. In the distance, it was a figure of dominance because of its sheer size. As he drove within a quarter of a mile of Mara, all the crows landed on its branches. It was now obvious to him that they led him to this location. But why?

He arrived at the foot of this great tree and stopped. Solomon turned off the engine and sat in his car for a few moments trying to understand the reason why he was chasing the annoying birds, but more specifically why they led him here. The driver's side door opened, he stepped out and began to stare above at the massive limbs that stretched out from the huge trunk; they extended out at least three or four car lengths in all directions. The shade these enormous limbs created was dark because Mara blocked out every inch of the sun with its display of strength and density. Its sheer mass was impressive.

His eyes began to focus on the crows as they gathered in one area but now were eerily silent. They were perched on limbs above him and high enough that he could not reach them. After a moment of pause, a piece of fruit fell out of the darkness and landed directly in front of his feet. It was as though the birds waited for him to make a move towards something sacred. The crows collectively held their breath, so to speak, in anticipation of his connection with the gift that lay before him.

He stepped forward and reached down to take it. The skin was fuzzy like a peach but firm and leathery. Even though the shade of the tree dampened the colors, he could see the interesting swirl of crimson red and deep yellow throughout its outer covering. Solomon thought it was strange that it felt weighty like a brick. The aroma was dense and he brought it closer to his nose for a deep inhale. It was sweet like the purest honey with pungent sour notes as well. He was attracted to its uniqueness and wanted to take another sniff, but he also couldn't stand the offensive undertones.

He must have been caught in a momentary trance because when he looked up at the crows they were nowhere to be found. His eyes glanced to his left and his right, but they were gone. They disappeared without any sound of flapping wings like they were never there at all. The moment was so bizarre. But at least his discovery of this new find was worth the minor inconvenience. More importantly, it would not be the last time he came to Mara for anything.

~

He choked on the rotten bitter taste of this odd fruit. Not only did his tongue curl, but his nostrils flared from the warmth of its fumes that worked harmoniously with its pale flesh to repel his appetite for curiosity. It was appalling. But something about this substance demanded greater attention.

At first, he recalled the stern warning his father gave him as a child. If he consumed its aromatic flesh would it make him ill or was that simply a conservative warning from a parent who had no such knowledge? It caused him to pause and consider the possible consequences of eating this unique fruit. But something persuaded him against all that he was told as if a gentle breeze carried whispers from somewhere else. Coupled with the notion that he was led by the persistent crows to the tree for a purpose, Solomon made his decision. He cautiously only took two small bites.

After a few days, he documented his interesting findings so far. Contrary to his father's counsel, Solomon experienced no ill effects whatsoever. He was relieved and continued with his work.

He broke away from his intensive study routine for a refreshing breath of fresh air. The sprawling patio provided a beautiful view of the serene countryside fully illuminated by the brilliant sunshine. As his mind cleared with the faint aroma of fields scattered with thousands of wildflowers, he noticed something in the foreground. It looked like a crow struggling to fly that lay helpless on the grassy field. It must have been there long before he stepped outside. One of its wings was oddly outstretched while the other was tucked by its side. It was silent but had its beak open for some reason. It was obvious to Solomon that the bird was in distress.

Just as he was about to approach it, he noticed another crow flying towards the injured or sick bird. He continued to watch this scene play out.

As the second crow landed by its ill companion, he noticed a piece of Mara's fruit in its beak. A sizeable chunk with part of the colorful outer skin made it recognizable to him. Then it began to feed some of the fruit to the bird who needed help. It was like a mother who feeds her chicks before they can fly. He still couldn't tell what was wrong with it, but the crow was not well.

The feeding lasted for a few minutes as he remained seated and watched the birds interact. A few more crows suddenly arrived from out of the sky and landed around the first two, encircling them. They were all silent and watched the lame bird flutter its wings slowly. As it continued to move with new strength, the crow eventually was able to stand. Whatever it was that sickened it seemed to pass and it began to caw with a loud cry, renewed with great strength. Then the few birds that surrounded it began to join in the celebration with loud shrieks of their own. They shared a sense of camaraderie and a bond united them closely.

By now the crow appeared to regain its health and flapped its wings with full force as it lifted off into the sky. The others followed as well and flew away. Solomon stood there in awe of what he had just witnessed. He thought how odd and mysterious it was that this exchange rendered healing to the one that required it. *Was this fruit the source of such power?* He could not help but become deeply intrigued by this bizarre anomaly. He was captivated by what unfolded. Perhaps this was the very solution he was searching for.

During the week he continued his focus on Mara's fruit and tried to uncover its secret. *Does it affect only birds? Is there a connection between this tree, its fruit, and these crows?* Many unanswered questions plagued his mind, but he was not going to forget the promise he made to his father. He will somehow use his experience and insight to find a cure for the sickness that took both of his parents.

And just as he committed his efforts and his life to his calling, he would discover something so rare and powerful that it would change the course of life for generations to come. He didn't come to these findings alone. These crows that guarded Mara were the difference. And of course, the mysterious fruit as well, which he named Cura.

~

Time spilled into the following month since he witnessed the mysterious crow incident. The exchange bothered him and it ate his time pondering the anomaly like a tapeworm devours nourishment. Something just wasn't normal about these birds. He decided to visit Mara once again and investigate. He wasn't exactly sure what his undertaking was, but he couldn't ignore the fascinating incident that unfolded during that afternoon.

As he drove through the countryside towards his destination, it felt as though the majestic tree invited him from a distance, just as one lures with enticement. His eyes began to focus on it across the plains. Bold in its stance and strong in its display, Mara never disappointed with such a fortress-like presence. He parked beneath the stretch of thick branches and the shade immediately provided comfort from the heat of the day.

As he stepped out from the car and stood there in awe, the crows began to heckle, muttering between themselves. He looked up into the midst of the tree—the crow's den. They were all separated as if they held assigned positions perched throughout Mara and its vast network of branches. The inquisitive man studied them for a moment. It was a staring contest of sorts between his curious eyes and the many crows that seemed to stare right back.

His attention focused on the tree itself. He looked closely at the bark. He realized the depth of its grain was infused with deep yet vibrant colors that could only be noticed during a close examination. Very thin slivers of crimson red, brilliant green, sky blue, canary yellow, and pale brown were visible within the tree's flesh. They were almost intertwined to form a unity. Just as if one could see a person's hair color from a few feet away, but when the eyes are a few inches away strands of varied color could be seen.

Solomon felt as though the bark contained an amazing life source that emitted from within. He pressed his hand lightly against it. *Is the tree breathing?* There was a subtle and slight pulsating movement his touch detected. A heartbeat; lungs that inhaled and exhaled; a pulse of life that emanated from Mara. It was remarkable.

Solomon decided to sit and rest awhile as he gathered his thoughts. He sat quietly at the base of the trunk. The shady covering seemed like a heavy canopy of an evening that drowns out radiant sunshine. He soaked in the beauty that surrounded him in every direction and expected nothing else except moments of peace and serenity. After all, what could you expect from a tree? That's where he was wrong.

It must have been almost half an hour when he whispered something.

"This is ridiculous. Why did I even come out here again?"

He quickly turned his head to see who was there. A distinct voice answered him, but he saw no one.

"Hello? Who's there?" he asked.

This time he stood up and looked around the large trunk as if someone was hiding behind it. He heard a voice again speak to him. After a quick search, he realized he was alone. Then he turned his head up into the tree's expanse above him. All he could see were a mass of crows studying him.

"Anyone up there?" he asked once more.

Once again, a voice responded as if a person stood right beside him.

"I am here," said the voice with a deep grainy, hollow tone.

A sound not heard anywhere else carried the weight of authority and reverberations similar to deep waves created by a thousand cellos.

"Why have you returned?"

Solomon continued to look in all directions, puzzled.

"Look. I don't know where you are, but please show yourself to me?" he asked.

"But I already have. You are speaking with the tree you came to rest by."

Solomon frowned and quickly stepped away from the tree in disbelief. He continued to search with his eyes for the person who was hiding.

"Alright. Enough with the games. Show yourself!" he said in frustration.

"Solomon. This is me, Mara. Do not be so surprised. I can do great and many things. Conversations are not difficult to have," the voice said.

"But. But you're a tree," said Solomon. "That's impossible."

"You have never spoken with a tree before? Not all of us choose to speak and I am the wisest of them all. Consider yourself in the best company."

"Alright. So, my ears don't hear you but my mind does. How is this possible?" he asked.

"Solomon. Do not be so concerned with the how, but instead choose to embrace the why," said Mara. "Come now and sit before me and I will tell you of so many wonderful things. Let us begin with that fruit you have in your pocket."

He reached into his jacket pocket and removed the fruit kept in a folded brown paper bag that he brought with him. It was the piece he was given last time he visited the tree. It was half of its original size, missing a portion used from tasting and research. He held it out in his hand as if to show it to the tree. But Mara knew it was already there, concealed in his pocket when he arrived. It was interesting to him that the fruit had no decay whatsoever.

"How did you know that I brought this? It was hidden in my pocket? How can you see at all?" he asked curiously.

"I know and I see, Solomon. Now, let me begin." Mara said.

Solomon rested by the tree for hours. He listened and he paid attention to every ounce of information relayed from Mara. Once he realized there were volumes of details to consume, he retrieved a tablet and a pen from his car. At times, he stood and paced. Other times, he laid on his back beneath Mara's shade paralyzed in awe about its beautiful strength and vast wisdom. He listened intently and recorded all of the specifics.

Mara began with the power of its fruit. The mystery of its nourishment was explained in great detail so that he could pass this on to others who would listen. Methods of preservation and extraction were documented for their direct influence on the human body. How it could be unlocked to express its fullest potential and why it mattered, was revealed to him.

The tree also explained the great disease that consumed his parents would bring distress to the land of Esid Arapym in the coming years and generations that would follow. It would wreak havoc in families and bring death to many homes. But the Cura fruit could bring life to some. It would require the right person and a costly sacrifice.

The power within the fruit and its nectar was only a component of the great mystery of its healing in humans. It also required the willingness of someone selfless to offer himself or herself to another person—a grantor. To trade health with someone else—a recipient—and to rescue that individual from illness for the rest of their years. By doing so, this brought certain a specific illness and eventually death to the grantor. This could only take place one time in a grantor's life. Only one opportunity to trade sorrows with another.

A thirty-third birthday was the sole day upon which a grantor had to accomplish this task. Mara explained the importance of this age and how it was the pivotal date in someone's existence. The moment in a human timeline representing the age of atonement; the beginning of one's maturity into matters of wisdom, deepest love, and the day of calling to reap a harvest sacrifice. Mara called it the date of significance: the day one becomes thirty-three years old.

So, on someone's thirty-third birthday this magnificent gift was available to offer and became the singular date in one's history that could change the course of someone's life forever. However, due to the permanent and deadly sting of this life transfer very few would decide to drink the nectar in this manner. Mara foresaw the fact that few would receive this amazing and mysterious gift.

Solomon returned to his home with a wealth of knowledge. He immediately began to formulate all of this important information he received from Mara into organized journals. He spent many hours into the late evening and early morning documenting every detail. Each line and every word was recorded with great care.

Over time, he formulated unique nectar from Cura fruit just as it was outlined in his notes. He also founded an organization dedicated to the preservation of Mara and the crows, the Cura fruit, and all that was related to this mystery of hope. And those few who were chosen to uphold the assignment of protecting and carrying out its sacred power would later be known as The Council of Elders.

After a rather successful endeavor of completing his father's desire and upholding his word to help find a method to help fight against the disease of the land, Solomon married Louise and had two children. They raised them on their estate and lived quiet yet happy lives.

After Solomon's passing, the traditions of the council continued. However, the mystery that surrounded the council's aim had become nothing more than a fable to many in Esid

Arapym. It was rare, but over the many decades that followed, a few people still believed in the mysterious, sacred nectar's power and accepted the offer to drink it. The purpose was to give another person healing. It would be a fatal gift of life; it would be known as the wish transfer.

CHAPTER 3

The Appointment

The invitations were mailed over two weeks earlier to twelve people. The list of witnesses to her momentous day was carefully written by Samantha. Her thirty-third birthday was soon approaching and she knew exactly what that meant to her. The individuals she selected were significant to her and they would be invited to participate in a once-in-a-lifetime event at her home.

She also knew exactly what was at stake. She would trade her health for affliction with Stillwhorm Syndrome at some point in her life. The onset of her illness could begin immediately or it could happen months in the future. Maybe even years. However, the wish recipient would experience healing from any sickness, Stillwhorm or any other, for the rest of their life or a powerful immunity would be imparted. It would become the recipient's imputed destiny.

One month before her special day, a member of the Council of Elders, the group dedicated to preserving the sacred drink and its origin, contacted her. As part of everyone's upcoming thirty-third birthday, the council used birth records to follow each resident of Esid Arapym and their role began by contacting those who perhaps would offer their birthday wish for another person. Most of the time the council rarely discovered anyone ready to exchange the power of permanence with another. Or, in some cases, some didn't live long enough to see their thirty-third birthday. Like Russell who died in his thirty-second year.

The member of the Council always made a personal appearance to the potential wish grantor. It was no different for Samantha. She received a courtesy call the day before and she expected someone to arrive that afternoon. It was "the appointment."

The doorbell rang and a nervousness welled up within her. She answered the door.

"Good afternoon, Samantha Parsons."

The elder spoke with a voice that was high in an elevated pitch, very proper and distinguished. His eyes were tired behind his round eyeglasses and he wore a formal business suit loosely over his heavy build. His dark gray hair was parted to one side.

"My name is Mr. Harshom and I am with the Council of Elders."

He reached out his right hand to greet her.

"Good afternoon," Samantha kindly accepted and shook his hand gently. "Please come in."

"Thank you," he said as he stepped into her welcoming home.

"Please have a seat," she said as she pointed to her dining room table.

"I will."

His voice carried a sense of authority and a weight of tenure. Mr. Harshom placed his briefcase by his side on the floor as he took his seat at the dinner table. Samantha sat across from him with great anticipation.

"May I get you some tea or coffee?" she said pointing toward the kitchen.

"Not at all. Thanks," he quickly stated. "I would like to entertain the heart of the matter today if you don't mind."

"Sure," Samantha spoke with acceptance.

"As you know, your thirty-third birthday is one month away. I've come to settle the decision you would like to make concerning the opportunity for a wish transfer."

His words were matter-of-fact and deliberate.

"In short, my presence today requires your decision. Your choice to accept or to reject the sacred nectar."

He reached into his weathered leather briefcase and retrieved a file and placed it on the table in front of them. He began to sort through the documents.

"Do you understand the thirty-third birthday wish?"

"Yes. I understand and I would like to accept the Council's offer for a sacred wish," she said nervously and unrehearsed.

Mr. Harshom stopped fussing with the paperwork and looked directly into her eyes.

"Samantha, are you sure about this?"

His stark response and reaction startled her. It caught her by surprise.

"Have you considered the consequences?"

He waited for her reply. She fumbled with her hands and avoided eye contact as she searched for her words.

"Samantha!" he spouted abruptly. "You will die."

"Yes!"

She boldly answered immediately as she stared back.

"Yes, I completely understand what will happen to me."

She shifted in her seat. She was made to feel discomfort purposely by his interrogation. He wanted to be sure about her intentions.

The elder shifted his attention back to the file and search for a specific document. He pulled his ink pen from inside of his coat pocket and pressed the top of it with his thumb. His hand-scribbled something on a tan notecard.

"I need you to attend a meeting at the address listed here. Monday evening at seven o'clock sharp. Will there be a conflict with your schedule?" he asked.

"Why do I need to go to this meeting?" she questioned. "I've already made up my mind to move forward with this. I've heard about these meetings. No one can persuade me to change my mind."

He looked at her puzzled and shrieked.

"Do you have a death wish, Samantha?"

"Why, no. No, I don't," she said confidently.

After a long and unusual pause, Mr. Harshom retracted the card and crumpled it before pushing it back into his briefcase. Samantha noticed his body language suggested he was agitated. He looked back at the opened file on the table and removed a glossy, silver sheet of paper. It was different from anything she had ever seen before. He set it on the table in front of her and then pulled something else out of his briefcase. It was a black case about the size of a small calculator. He placed it directly on the table in front of him and studied the object for several seconds.

"You must forgive me. I haven't done this in a very long while."

His voice was now saddened and a bit melancholy.

He held the case in one hand and with the other began to pull a thin tab on the side. It was a seal that held it together. Slowly, his hand removed the adhesive seal that held both sides of the case together. He placed the strand of thin tape into his briefcase and straightened the small container directly in front of his buttoned suit jacket. He stared at it for a few more seconds as it rested on the table's surface.

"Here we go, Samantha," he said as both of his hands took hold of it.

"What is this? A contract?" she asked, staring down at the blank document.

She looked puzzled because it had no words, only a small circle outlined in black towards the bottom.

Mr. Harshom separated the container into two sides, and he set them on the table with the newly exposed insides facing upward. He said nothing. Not yet. There was a pearly white pen set inside of a mold that lined half of the case. The lining was a deep red, like crimson. He removed the pen and held it in front of his eyes as he squinted. The pen looked like it was made from pearl white marble and it had a gold cap on each end. The sun's rays caused a shimmering reflection of light against it as it peered through the window.

"Take this pen and do as I say," said Mr. Harshom methodically and stretching the words as if he was directing specific movements.

He handed it to her across the dining room table. She reached out to accept the pen and froze until he spoke again. Her eyes were stuck in a gaze, a frown of mild confusion.

He slid the silver sheet of paper closer to her until the bottom was nearly touching her. The circle side was down, close to her. She stared down onto the blank surface and waited for his direction.

"Pay close attention, Samantha," he urged. "This is ceremonial in nature and requires your utmost respect."

"I understand," she replied with concern in her tone.

"You will notice an empty agreement in front of you having one circle at the bottom. Correct?" he asked.

"Yes. I do."

"You are about to signify your willingness to partake of the sacred nectar," he added. "Now, remove both gold caps from each end of this pen you now possess."

Samantha held the center with one hand and with her free hand removed one cap, then the other. She set them down beside the blank sheet. One end was a tip of an ink pen used for writing and the other end was a lancet. After a short visual inspection, her eyes returned to his face.

"Now what?" she said calmly.

"Take the sharp end and prick your fingertip. The finger of your choice," he said as he raised both of his palms to her and wiggled his fingers slightly.

Samantha was uncomfortable with his creepy mannerisms but continued. She held the lancet side downward firmly in her hand and quickly pierced the thumb of her empty hand. The blood began to seep out and form a very small bubble on her skin.

He blurted.

"Now take your thumb and press it onto the surface of the agreement. Be sure you keep your blood inside of the circle only."

She placed the pad of her bleeding thumb onto the form exactly as he said. And before she pulled it up from the page, something appeared slowly on the surface. It was a symbol of some kind.

"Yes. Yes," he said as the document transformed.

Mr. Harshom began to nod his head in acceptance as he chanted the following words:

"You have answered the call. From your heart so deep within, you embrace a moment meant for those who wish something sacred. Sacred for two lives: yours and another of your choice.

You need not answer at this moment. Save your chosen one for that day upon which you trade sorrows, my dear."

She heard his voice but kept staring intently at the image that appeared. The silver piece of paper now turned an ivory white shade with a distressed appearance, similar to hairline fractures on stone, and a black image above her blood imprint. It was an image of a crow with its wings folded over each other and its head facing forward. Her initials in crimson red, "SP" appeared vertically, "S" above the "P," in the center of the crow's chest area.

"What is this?" she asked. "These are my initials. So, this represents me?"

"Samantha, this document reveals the wish grantor by their initials. The blood, your blood, is recognized within the page's link to the Council and all of the bloodlines in Esid Arapym. This is your destiny and you have chosen it," he answered. "Once you have placed your signature below your imprint, at the bottom of this page your decision will be complete. This agreement will now be filed with the council for future reference and I will no longer need your time this afternoon."

He stood up and held out his open hand to receive the signed agreement.

"So, now what happens?" she asked.

Her words held some bitterness as she turned the pen upside down and hastily signed her name as instructed. Perhaps because of the realization of what she committed to. She slowly handed him the document and the pen after her signature was provided.

Mr. Harshom stood and placed his open briefcase upon the table. He carefully inserted the folder with all of its documents, and the pen secured into its case back inside then fastened the latch securely. His day's work was done.

He faced her with a reassuring smile proudly on display.

"I will see you on your birthday, here at your lovely home. You and the guests of your choice," said the elder.

He walked to the front door as Samantha remained sitting at the table, somewhat in disbelief and dazed at what had just transpired. She realized her guest had already led himself to the door and as he turned the doorknob to open it, her attention immediately focused on him.

"Uh…thank you, Mr. Harshom," she blurted out quickly after a slight hesitation.

He paused. The elder stood facing the door for a moment then he turned to face her. His eyes had transformed into windows of his soul, something she had never seen in anyone before. A seriousness emitted through them and also something mysterious. His words broke the eerie silence between them both.

"You have no idea what has allowed this benefit to flow through your wish. Please revere the power of Mara and its sacred fruit. The tree from which all good things flow has no purpose other than offering those who willingly sacrifice themselves a portion of the inheritance. An opportunity to partner with Mara for the legacy upon which it exists. Of which the crows also become vessels and instruments of the calling. Please show reverence."

Samantha appeared to fall into a trance by his speech. Her eyes were frozen in a cold stare. Something in her synchronized with the elder's explanation; she stepped into a new level of understanding.

"Good day," said Mr. Harshom as he walked out and closed the door behind him.

She slowly stood from her seat, motionless and fazed. Her eyes stared down at her pricked thumb and then over to a nearby picture of Dominic that rested on a desk. It began to sink into

36

deeper levels of her heart and in her mind. The finality of her decision continued to weigh on her for the rest of the day and into the evening.

Mr. Harshom was satisfied by his encounter with Samantha and the results made for a thrilling day. He stepped into his car and returned to the council chambers.

He was an odd man. But, given the nature of his position and his immense responsibility to preserve such a legacy that surrounded the sacred fruit, he acted with the utmost respect towards these matters. And that was vital. He was on the current end of a line of elders who served from the origin of the Council once it was established by Solomon Childs long ago.

Although it was an honor to be selected by the Council to serve in this capacity, it consumed one's life by extreme devotion that was required. Most of the elders that served did not have families of their own. This included Mr. Harshom. He remained at the chambers most of his day preparing for a day such as the one that just took place. His sleeping quarters were also located on the grounds and he had other members who would tend the facility. This enabled him to devote every moment to his calling and his care for all things related to the Cura fruit, Mara, and…the crows.

CHAPTER 4

Thirty-third Birthday

Samantha called from across the hallway to her son as she walked from her bedroom toward his, putting on her earrings.

"Do you have your shoes on yet?"

"Yeah, Mommy," Dominic replied as he sat on his bedroom floor enjoying a pop-out book. He was dressed in a handsome outfit along with his brown casual boots. They were his favorite article of footwear.

She walked in and made a fuss about how special he looked. His grin and gleam in his eyes planted a special memory in her heart. Over the years since he was born, she had stored volumes of similar ones for later use. She just added another to her collection.

It was half-past the three when her first guests had arrived at her home. They were James and Judy Clark, the ice cream shop owners. Although the invitations designated Samantha's birthday celebration to commence at four o'clock, she knew some folks would arrive early.

Shortly after, the remaining guests along with Mr. Harshom had arrived. The twelve invitees were present and were dressed in formal party attire. This was an auspicious occasion. They all gathered in the living room and enjoyed hors d'oeuvres with light conversation. The mood was upbeat and vibrant. The house was decorated with party decorations, including clusters of pink and yellow balloons that were placed in many areas of the interior. Soft piano music softly filled the atmosphere.

Samantha made her way to each of the attendees with Dominic by her side. She greeted and thanked each one of them for being there. They expressed their gratitude for being invited and wished her a happy birthday. Each guest brought a gift for Samantha and placed them on the dining room table. Of course, they were delighted with the possibility of being the recipient of her wish transfer. But it would only be one person; this potentially once-in-a-lifetime moment could not be shared amongst many or a few. No, only one individual would be the recipient of this selfless act.

At the top of the four o'clock hour, Mr. Harshom began to make an announcement.

"Would everyone please gather around the dining room table as we shall begin with today's auspicious occasion? It is time to commence with the ceremony."

The guests, Samantha, and Dominic created a semi-circle around the table and faced Mr. Harshom. Before his announcement, he removed the contents of a black travel case and set them on the table. They were two objects. The first was a smoky gray, crystal chalice with an ornate decorative stem and a gold-lined rim. The second was a rectangular-shaped stone-like object, eleven inches tall and its girth was similar to a brick commonly used in the construction of outdoor furnaces. The stone was smooth and matte black. Its top side had a spout but was sealed so that its precious contents could not spill. They were not ordinary pieces of dishware. It was apparent to all attendees that these elements were meant for unique circumstances. And today was as unique as could be.

"All in attendance. Welcome. You are present to help celebrate Samantha Parsons' thirty-third birthday. You all, guests by specific invitation, have one chance in thirteen to be the sole recipient of her wish transfer."

Mr. Harshom spoke with a voice of a dignitary.

"As an official member of the Council of Elders, I have been appointed to officiate Samantha's thirty-third birthday event."

Every heart in that dining room was frozen in a state of paralysis due to their huge anticipation. Every eye was intently focused on his actions. Mr. Harshom did not loosen his navy blue necktie, even though it appeared to be tightly wound and pinching his vocal cords. He continued to move his hands as he delivered every word with precision, occasionally making eye contact with Samantha's guests.

"Esid Arapym stands upon a pillar of the community. Immovable and strengthened by those who live within its vast borders."

His high-pitched voice was unsettling, but their complete attention was worth every audible tonal offense he delivered.

"You all understand the importance of this appointment. I don't find any reason to deliver such an explanation. But I will say Samantha has chosen the most powerful act anyone could participate in. Her actions will soon demonstrate to the Council and this community what it means to offer the ultimate sacrifice."

To say you could hear echoes of silence would be an understatement. The tension began to heighten and consume the air with its blunt force. Mr. Harshom's hands reached down to the stone-like flask set in front of him and began to inspect the seal with his fingertips. Samantha could have used this moment to take several, deep cleansing breaths, but there was not much time remaining. The anxiety welled up from within like a rising creek beneath pouring rainfall, ready to overflow. She clutched her hands together and wore a nervous smile out of courtesy. Here gaze shuffled between those in attendance quickly as if she had a short attention span. Dominic stood quietly and calmly at her side. He studied every movement and every detail that was present before him.

The elder broke the silence once again as he turned his eyes toward her.

"Samantha Parsons. Would you please take your place at my side, dear?"

She nodded and moved through the small crowd from where she stood, directly across the table from the elder and over to his position. She faced him and paid close attention.

Then his voice became deliberately monotone and Mr. Harshom spoke in a slow tempo.

"Samantha. You have answered the call. From your heart so deep within, you embrace a moment meant for those who wish something sacred. Sacred for two lives: yours and another of your choice."

He frowned in deep concentration as he stared directly into the face of the kind figure before him.

"Samantha," he repeated her name in a higher pitch. "Samantha, who have you selected to be the recipient of your sacred wish transfer?"

Before the gathering of eager souls, ready to hear their name exhaled from the lips of their host, the guests anticipated her next words. This was the moment in their lives meant for a possible weight to be lifted; a day that could alter the course of their lives. But whom would she choose? Which name will she speak into destiny?

Within seconds, Samantha exhaled and spoke as she covered her heart with both hands.

"With my sacred wish, I choose Dominic, my son."

The room's tension immediately diffused with the delivery of her announcement. A quiet calm entered instead as some wore the look of defeat, disappointment, or relief. All eyes shifted to Dominic who stood across the table from his mother and the elder. Samantha called to him and held out her arms for him to fall into. He wasn't sure what just happened, but he felt reassurance from his mother and that's all that mattered.

Dominic dashed into his mother's arms and embraced her as she knelt. Her tears were proof that the love between a mother and her child was unbreakable and unstoppable. She soon realized the ceremony had to continue, so she let her son go and smiled at him as she stood. He smiled right back.

Mr. Harshom wasted no time. As the group watched Dominic stand beside his mother, the elder carefully removed the seal to the special flask. He set the mahogany wax, seal material next to the chalice and with both hands lifted the stone-like object to his face. As the spout was held beneath his nose, he took a deep breath in to inhale the aroma now emitting from the container. He closed his eyes as his senses were overtaken by the sweet notes of the nectar. His actions confirmed to the gathering of guests that the elder was a strange and an odd man.

Samantha looked at him with curiosity. She wondered why he was so drawn to this mysterious drink. He was captivated by it somehow. And after an awkward pause, he exhaled as if he held his breath for minutes at a time. He lowered the container towards the chalice and began to pour a liquid into its emptiness. The drink was smooth and looked like molten, silky liquefied metal. Deep hues of burnt orange made it unlike anything else. Mr. Harshom poured and filled the chalice halfway to the gold brim then placed the empty flask back on the table. He seemed satisfied with his minor accomplishment. Almost as though he achieved something grand up until now. But the climactic moment was about to rise to its peak.

The elder took the chalice and held it between Samantha and Dominic. He uttered a few more words.

"Now you must consider the agreement you have made and honor it, Samantha. This is your moment, for both of you."

He turned slightly toward her and offered her the drink. She accepted and held it up to her mouth. She waited to drink and looked down at her son. Her voice was tender and soothing as she spoke.

"I do this for you. Because I love you and my love has no end. No matter what happens to me, nothing can separate my love for you."

Then her hands brought the rim of the chalice against her lips and she sipped some of the nectar. Immediately, she felt a rush of warmth throughout her bones and her vascular system. It overwhelmed her taste buds that sent alarming signals to her brain. The drink was marred with bitterness, but the aroma had the sweetest effect on her. She made a facial expression that suggested to everyone she couldn't take another sip because of its rude flavor, but also strangely satisfying. Mixed emotions flared. She welled up tears and smiled with joyful bliss.

"Now offer it to Dominic," instructed Mr. Harshom.

"Here, Dommie. Just take a small sip and don't worry," she assured her son.

Dominic took the cup from her mother's hands and slowly brought it closer to his face so that he could smell it. He was very cautious but suddenly the sweet aroma planted a grin on his worried face. Relieved, he quickly took a sip from the chalice and his eyes opened wide. He experienced the same effects as his mother moments before and it caught him off guard. Then he took another drink and finished the nectar that remained.

Samantha burst out into tears and she took the chalice from him and set it on the table. She fell to her knees and held him. The guests were now witnesses to a ceremony that rarely occurred. They all applauded and Mr. and Mrs. Clark wept happy tears for Dominic. They both knew what this meant for him and for that blessing they were relieved.

But no one was happier than Samantha. There was no comparison to her level of unexplainable joy knowing that Dominic would not have to endure the terrible illness that took his father's life the year before. He would never become a victim to any sickness or disease, for that matter. Because the exchange was accomplished. The wish transfer was made. It was permanent and immediately covered her son's life. It wasn't a life serum that evaded mortality, but rather a covering from all threatening forms of sickness.

And for Samantha, calamity was lurking around every corner. A demise caused by Stillwhorm was certain. She traded her life for his. It was the optimum outcome she chose for their lives together. There was absolutely no way she could bear the pain to see him ever become sick and eventually die. It was waiting for him in the bloodline. But she made sure it would not happen. Even if it would cost her own life.

And what no one inside her home could see was a garrison of crows that flew above the home in a wide circular pattern. A few others were positioned on the perimeter perched on nearby trees to watch from the ground level. The crows remained diligently on task. They were there because of Samantha and her wish. Guardians that offered a seal of protection and a show of force against anything that would dare to interrupt this important ceremony. They knew of the evil that was present; it waited in the shadows for an opportunity to bring destruction.

Mr. Harshom gathered the elements and secured them in his case as everyone began to settle down. He approached Samantha and Dominic before he left.

"I am grateful for you allowing me the opportunity to witness and to conduct this important ceremony. Thank you."

"No, thank you for your help today," she replied as she gratefully shook his hand.

He looked down and patted Dominic on his head.

"You did very well, Master Dominic. Terrific job."

"Thanks," Dominic said sheepishly. He had no idea of the magnitude of what just took place. But one day he would.

The elder turned and walked away carrying his case. His role was fulfilled that day. He would return to the Council with a complete report of what occurred at the Parsons residence and with an empty sacred nectar flask. The special container would then be refilled and sealed just as it was before. Waiting and ready for the next wish transfer.

~

That evening was as special as any other she could remember. The internal serenity of her son's health assurance cradled her mind. Sleepless nights were left in the past. Samantha's dread of her son's potential threat from Stillwhorm became insignificant. But the previous struggle was overwhelming to her; unsettling emotions develop from within a mother's existence when a threat is presented and a powerful sense of protection for their children rises.

Mothers have an innate ability—an instinct—to protect their children. From the beginning throughout the unfolding of time, mothers formed a loving bond with their children during pregnancy and there was nothing in existence that could dissolve such ties. They will fight and they will nurture with whatever sacrifice is required. It is a purely magnificent connection they possess.

Yes, Samantha slept peacefully that evening. After sharing some laughs with Dominic while she read one of his favorite books, his weary eyes fell victim to slumber. She tucked him gently beneath warm covers and leaned over his face slowly so as not to wake him.

She whispered to her son.

"Goodnight, Dommie. I love you."

She kissed his forehead and held back a flood of her tears.

As she left his room, her eyes shed more emotion than she had in a while. The tables had now turned, but she felt they had done so in her favor—under her control. Sure, sweet Dominic had a clean bill of health for the rest of his life, but that didn't come at a meaningless price. No, it cost her. It cost her the very existence she would have enjoyed. She imagined the pain that was about to inflict misery upon her flesh and tissues. Stillwhorm Syndrome was a death sentence for her. Still, she would have it no other way. The soothing thought of her healthy boy was all the medicine in the world that she needed.

She loved him more than anything. It was her love that traded lives with her little boy; a life for a life. It was her love that he would forever carry in his heart for the rest of his days.

~

The next morning, a firm knock on the door interrupted Samantha as she was folding a fresh batch of laundry in the utility room. Dominic was playing outside in the garden and kept to himself most of the time. She put down the towel she began to fold and headed for the front door. She glanced out of the side window to see who it was. To her surprise, it was a man she had not recognized.

"Good afternoon," she greeted the visitor after she opened the door.

"Hello, Samantha Parsons," he said with a formal voice. "My name is Clyde. Clyde Serwhoven and I represent the Office of State."

He waited for her to extend her hand before offering his. She was apprehensive, but after a slight pause, she reached and shook hands with the stranger. Samantha was a bit surprised and unsure why he was there to see her.

"How do you know my name? Have we met somewhere before?" she asked.

"I'm afraid we haven't had the pleasure until this moment."

The man answered her as he smiled, but only with his mouth and none of his other features joined in. He was a large wiry man who stood close to seven feet tall and he wore a charcoal gray suit. His lanky frame was obvious because of the slim-fitting clothing. His lightless eyes were piercing and became a stark contrasting feature against his pasty, pale skin tone. The blonde, stringy eyebrows across his brow were barely noticeable and his short, light-colored hair was parted neatly to one side—almost too perfect. The chapped lips beneath a pointy nose became obvious because of his perfectly shaven skin. He was an interesting person to look at.

"May I come in?"

She paused then agreed.

"Yes, forgive me. Please come in," she stepped aside to allow his entrance into the living room. "Have a seat."

"Thank you."

Clyde strolled over to a large chair across from the sofa and sat down. He began to assess the immediate surroundings and instantly noticed an abundance of family pictures nestled in many places. As he adjusted himself in his seat, he seemed quite at ease in his new environment. But it was almost as if he waited for this singular moment to occur for many years.

"So, please tell me why you are here," Samantha asked as she sat on a sofa across from him.

Clyde rested his right leg over his left and placed both hands calmly over his right thigh. He felt it was necessary to ensure his comfort before he answered her question. He was odd, but cordial nonetheless.

"I oversee the residents of Esid Arapym concerning their adherence to specific laws. At least those concerning mystic realms or are borderline fictitious. Furthermore, I allocate the necessary resources within the context of unusual behavior and assess any violations," he said with a cold stare.

She turned her head slightly to one side trying to understand what he meant by violations and if that was the reason for his visit. Her countenance gave her suspicions away.

"Now I assure you, Samantha, my presence here is merely informal. Let's just say a visit of vital introductions. You're not in any trouble," he said. "I merely want to introduce myself to the one who just yesterday completed a wish transfer. Happy belated birthday, by the way."

Samantha forced herself to grin and thanked him. Something about Clyde was unsettling.

"You're quite the talk of the town. You've nearly attained the status of celebrity in these parts," he said.

"And how do you know about this?" she asked.

"A man in my position is quite familiar with a great many things."

His voice began to become testy. She could sense a stiff pride about him. He continued.

"Under the scope of my position include all matters concerning unorthodox wish transfers directed by the Council.

I despise such acts performed outside of the parameters of normalcy and tread firmly upon those who believe in such nonsense."

"Nonsense?" she quickly asked. "What do you mean?"

"Allow me to be blunt, Samantha. You're a smart woman, right?" he said with a smirk.

He unfolded his legs and sat upright.

"I wish to ban all acts surrounding the Council and its traditional methods. These so-called wish transfers are questionable and I intend to investigate each one. Yours just so happens to be fresh being that it was only yesterday." He quickly changed subjects. "How is your son?"

"He's fine," she replied. "Why do you ask?"

"I know that he was the recipient of your wish, is that correct?" he nodded in anticipation of her answer.

"Yes."

"Yes, yes. So, is he feeling well? Was he ill before this event?" he asked.

"Mr. Serwhoven," she said but was interrupted.

"Clyde. You may call me Clyde," he insisted.

"I'm afraid it's time for you to leave," she said as she stood abruptly.

Clyde stood to his feet and adjusted his suit jacket.

"Very well. I will be in touch."

"There's no need," she said adamantly.

He took a few steps across the room towards the door, then stopped to say one more thing.

"I'm sorry for your loss. Russell was a very good man."

"Stop it. That's enough. You never knew my husband," Samantha struck back.

Her emotion rose from a place of grief and of terrible pain. His towering frame turned and looked down upon her angry eyes.

"I most certainly did," he said barely above a whisper. "A courageous man with strength and honor. Too bad he fell to the clutches of Stillwhorm Syndrome so early in his life."

He turned and continued to make his exit. His steps were long and calculated. As he opened the door and stepped outside, he exhaled his final words.

"Stillwhorm Syndrome. Probably the most perfect disease."

Samantha rushed to the door as he walked out and slammed it behind him. She stared out of the side window as her left hand secured the latch on the door. She trembled with anger. He walked down the driveway and got into his vehicle. She made sure he drove off before she walked away from the window. Her eyes were filled with rage.

"He's got some nerve," she said angrily. "I'm watching you, creep."

"Mommy, you talking to yourself?"

Dominic asked as he hopped inside of the kitchen from the backyard. He made his way to the cookie jar and grabbed a handful of snacks.

"Hey, mister. Save some room for lunch," she playfully said to her son.

His entrance broke the spell of Clyde's lingering foul mood. He skipped back outside quickly and acknowledged his mother with a single word.

"Yup."

His innocence whipped up a chuckle and a smile as she lovingly gazed at her son. It did not matter what just took place in her home. There wasn't anything that could permanently distract her from her sweet boy's sense of lofty joy. A moment with Dominic could create a lasting peaceful afterglow every single time.

CHAPTER 5

He steadied his shaky hands before proceeding. This would require undivided and sure concentration. Every aspect of the ritual that pertained to the wish transfer was sacred and must be elevated to the highest regard of respect. He held his breath for a few moments to clear his mind. With a slow and steady exhale, Mr. Harshom was ready.

The dimly lit service room within the chamber did not detract from his ability to stay on task. All sources of light had to be kept to a minimum during this process. He began to hum a tune that looped in his mind. It was a melody he learned as a child that helped him through some difficult times later in his middle-aged life. He glanced around the room one last time. *Yes,* he thought, *the large assortment of candles surrounding the perimeter seems to be perfect lighting for this task.* Then, he began.

He stood over a vessel hewn from stone the size of an enormous treasure chest. It was about as high as his waist. Its lid, fabricated from oak and stained with dark gray oils, protected the contents safely. There was no lock, but broad leather straps on both sides held the lid in place. A large bird symbol was carved on the top side and words were inscribed beneath it that read across the bottom:

WHERE DEATH AND LIFE COLLIDE

The straps were removed and he lifted the hefty lid off of the surface with both hands. It was carefully placed on its end upon the cold ground. Mr. Harshom peered inside the container's belly, but the darkness inside made it difficult to find the source of his task. He gingerly used both of his gloved hands to reach down into the blackness.

"Ah. There you are," he mumbled.

His hands carefully pulled upwards holding a lifeless crow.

"So, so precious are you."

His body turned gently and he crept towards a table as he held the crow. There on the surface was a unique box meant for the dead bird. And with the same caution he used to retrieve it, the elder placed the subject within the box that was lined with scarlet fabric. Next to the box was its lid. But before he enclosed the crow within its coffin, tradition required him to utter a speech.

Mr. Harshom cleared his throat and then coughed. He stared down upon the lifeless bird.

"You have made the journey, my friend. From being a guardian of Mara to a chosen vessel for a life-giving source. You are honored and your sacrifice has been recognized by all who reside here in Esid Arapym. Godspeed to you. Your task here is finished."

The elder took the lid and carefully set it onto the box. It was designed to fit snug and secure; no latches or locks were necessary. He let out a long exhale before picking it up. He secured it under is his left arm against his side. It was time to deliver it to the rightful recipient. He walked out of the chamber area and into his office. His somber mood was evident. He cared deeply for these rites and ceremonial deeds. But more for what they held and stood for.

~

53

Dani poured the hot water from the kettle into both her and Samantha's mugs. The teabags were in place ready for steeping.

"Thanks," said Samantha.

"Did you want anything else since I'm up?" Dani asked as she returned the kettle to the stove.

"No thanks."

"So, tell me more about this encounter with the creep," asked Dani.

Samantha had a frown across her brow as she searched for the right words.

"Creep is right. The guy was so odd and he just got under my skin," Samantha said as she shook her head in disgust. "It was like he was there to annoy me. It was strange."

Dani sat and began to stir her teabag that settled at the bottom of her mug.

"I wish I was here too. I would have said some things to set him off. He shouldn't have spoken to you like that. Especially about Russell," said Dani.

"It was a strange conversation."

Samantha took a sip of her steaming hot tea as she stared out into nowhere.

"I don't plan on seeing him anytime soon."

They sat for a few moments after a pause in their conversation about Clyde. Then Dani changed the mood with a more upbeat topic.

"So, how does it feel, Sam? I mean, on the inside. Do you feel any different after the wish thing?" Dani asked.

An instant smile graced Samantha's face.

"I'm so thankful I did that for Dommie. As difficult as it was, you know, to come to terms with the outcome for me and all. I know I did the right thing. And I'm going to make the rest of my days count. Whatever I have left with Dommie."

Dani's eyes and demeanor were overcome with sadness.

"You know I'm here for you. Whatever I can do."

Dani reached out her hand and grabbed Samantha's.

"I know. You're the best friend anyone could ask for, Dani," said Samantha with a smile. "I appreciate you. Honestly, I'm not sure what this whole thing will look like."

Samantha's face quickly showed the look of uncertainty and for the future pain she would endure just before those final days. She couldn't think of how much it will destroy her heart knowing she would be leaving him. But at the same time, this was better than watching him suffer from Stillwhorm Syndrome just like his father did. It was not what any parent should endure—watching their child wither away from disease. She did all that she could to remove him from that possibility, by taking his place.

The telephone rang and Samantha stood to reach for it.

"Hello? Oh, hello Mr. Harshom. How are you today? Sure. This afternoon at two would be fine. Alright. I will see you then. Goodbye."

She hung up the phone and returned to her seat next to Dani.

"So, that was Mr. Harshom. He wants to come by today to give me something," said Samantha.

"Did he tell you what it was?" Dani asked.

"No. He didn't. But he did say that it was important and a part of the wish process."

"Hmmm. Interesting," Dani said.

Samantha sipped her tea a couple of times as she stared off once again into nowhere. Dani could see that her friend was suddenly lost and held captive by her thoughts. She didn't want to ask, but she was curious as to what Samantha was wrestling with.

What Dani did not see was an uneasiness that suddenly crept in regarding this birthday wish situation. And that her friend was breaking down within small fragments already. How can a parent be able to prepare for certain death and leave her only child behind? There is no way to do so other than allow the trickle of death's anticipation to take small portions of her until it calls her by name. Mr. Harshom's phone call immediately brought those thoughts to the forefront of her mind.

Promptly at two o'clock, there was a knock at her door. Samantha anticipated the elder's arrival since his call earlier and she scurried over to let him in. Dani sat in the living room.

"Good afternoon, Mr. Harshom," said Samantha as she opened the door.

"Hello, Samantha. I do hope that I'm not intruding."

He was always polite and considerate. Mr. Harshom held an odd-looking object under his left arm tightly against his side. It was a dark box.

"No. Please come in."

"Thank you."

The elder walked into her home and greeted Dani with a hand wave. Then he quickly turned to Samantha.

"I don't want to keep you, but I brought you something."

Samantha smiled and offered him a chair, but he refused. The elder took the object from under his arm and held it with both hands in front of his waist. It was the size of a shoebox and was made of wood, stained with deep red oils, and had rough edges. Samantha's full name was hand-painted with white letters on top with a number in the lower right corner. The number was "32."

"This is yours. It represents the sacred wish transfer you've made and without its contents, you would not have been able to accomplish your transfer to Dominic."

Mr. Harshom's tone became serious and he looked down from his gaze at her, then stared intensely at the box he held.

"Without the sacrifice of *Thirty-two*, this would not have been possible."

Samantha turned to Dani with a confused look. Dani was caught off guard by her expression and shrugged her shoulders. Samantha quickly turned her eyes back to the elder who was still in a deadlock stare with the box he held.

"So, Mr. Harshom. What exactly is inside?" asked Samantha.

"Death, I'm afraid."

His tone was eerie.

"This one sacrificed it all. For you to gift Dominic."

Samantha became uneasy and she had a rush of chills flow through her body. He paused for a long while as she tried to comprehend the details of this moment. But her confused countenance revealed her insecurity.

"I'm sorry, but are you telling me there's a dead thing inside?"

His eyes immediately glared back at her face.

"Please show some respect. The dead thing, as you put it, is your appointed crow. This one has made the required sacrifice and we shall honor it with great reverence."

"I'm sorry. I'm thankful for everything you and the council have done for me. I mean no disrespect."

Samantha smiled and opened her hands as a gesture of gladly receiving his gift. Mr. Harshom was put at ease by her response. He handed the box to her.

"I thoroughly understand. Please take this and honor it appropriately," said the elder.

The crow appointed for Samantha's wish was required for the transfer to be implemented. One chosen crow from the guardianship of Mara had to fly to the Council of Elders the day

Samantha had signed her agreement in blood. It was brought into the chamber by Mr. Harshom where it was cared for until the day of her birthday. On the morning of the transfer day, it was fed its last meal and placed into the stone vessel to die.

This ceremonial death was an honor for these crows. They were devoted to Mara and everything meant for good. The wish transfer was deeply revered and for any one of them was considered a sacrifice towards a future for someone else.

Once the crow was placed into the stone vessel by the elder, the nectar was also set inside. A powerful blend of juice specifically directed by Mara was extracted by one of its most deadly fruits and used for this sole purpose. There were only several drops of this nectar put inside of a small cup because not much was required for a bird's death. Once everything was in place, the elder set the cover back on the stone vessel.

While in this dark and cold hollowed stone, the crow knew it had to ingest the nectar. It did not hesitate and within minutes of being covered, it breathed its last. There was no struggle or resistance at all, no shriek of pain or sorrow. The crow gave its life willingly by the fate of the mysterious nectar.

This portion of the ceremony made the elder deeply grieved. His adoration for these unique and exceptional creatures was unmatched. Although, he understood the complexity of the sacred wish transfer and this crow was vital to the process.

Mr. Harshom was caught in a momentary loss for words once the box was now in her possession. He caught himself and regained his composure.

"And how's Dominic doing?"

"Oh, quite well. He spends much of his time playing outside. He enjoys the outdoors and especially our garden," she answered.

"How delightful. May I see it?" asked the elder.

58

"Certainly. This way."

Samantha led Mr. Harshom to the backyard, still holding onto the box. He followed her and was amazed at the garden's beauty. He saw her son playing on the far side of the yard almost near the trees that created a wall where the woods began. The elder's grin seemed to be genuine. It was almost as if he experienced a moment of peace as he recorded the details of what he saw. But, what Samantha did not know or could not see was the very source of Mr. Harshom's instant happiness. It was a crow that was perched in a pine tree just on the other side of Dominic. It appeared to be watching the boy. Or, was it watching over him, as a bodyguard protects another?

"Thank you for allowing me to see this portion of paradise. I see Dominic is having the time of his life," he said as he turned to her. "And a full life he will have. I can let myself out. Thank you for your hospitality."

"You're welcome. And thanks again for bringing this by."

The elder waved at Dominic who looked his way and walked back into the house. Samantha stared down at the box she held and studied the details. The letters of her name were more vibrant beneath the light of the sun. She could see the tiny strokes of the paintbrush faintly within each letter. It suggested the great intention behind the one who prepared it. She had never seen anything like it. But, to honor the Council of Elders, she knew what had to be done.

~

The following week Samantha, Dominic, and Dani decided to take a day trip out to the open countryside. It was a much-needed disconnect from the swirling emotions regarding her birthday celebration.

It didn't take long to reach the outskirts of civilization. Bright-colored meadows blanketed the countryside for miles and for as far as the eye could see. It was a perfect outing for Samantha. When she asked Dani if she would enjoy the day with her and Dominic, there was no hesitation. Dani even insisted that she drive to allow them both the pleasure of a sweet journey.

The beauty and serenity of the scenery allowed Samantha's thoughts to be caressed by peace. She felt certain about her decision for the wish transfer to Dominic and the only reality that consumed her now was the thought about her leaving him soon. There was no mistaking separation by death; the permanence of her wish allocated certain incurable consequences to her humanity. It was a cold circumstance that began to loom inside of her tomorrows and whispered her name from a distance. A voice from somewhere that could not be ignored.

She suppressed the voice with an outpouring of more love to her son. Without knowing when her fate would ring her doorbell, Samantha bathed Dominic with her time and miniature acts of thoughtfulness. One of his favorite morning meals was wild berry hotcakes smothered in his mother's special fruit glaze topping. She offered it to him at least two or three times a week and he gladly accepted. Or most of the evenings he enjoyed his favorite storybook just before bedtime and Samantha acted out the animal characters with hand puppets. A mother's touch is magical and often brings comfort no other can provide. It was not difficult for her to labor in these sorts of ways for her Dommie. It was her delight to do so.

"Are you doing okay?" Dani called out to her backseat passenger. "I don't want you to get sick."

"I'm okay," Dominic said as he was preoccupied with a set of connectable toys. "Just playing."

Samantha glanced over her shoulder to Dominic with a sense of adoration.

"He's so smart. He'll do some amazing things with his life," said Samantha.

A pleasant ninety-minute drive brought them into a wonderland of escape. The rolling hillsides stretched for distances that seemed to span across time. Colors reserved for dreams of fantasy and times beyond exploded before their eyes. They could smell the plush fragrance of wildflowers and sweet notes that only come from well-manicured lawns. Their senses were in sheer delight and their moods were brightened by such a gracious day.

They found a dirt road and followed it from the main highway. It escorted them into more of an uncharted area, or so it felt. A mild sense of adventure stirred their curiosity and they felt led to enjoy this trip to its fullest. Bustling trees were scattered into the fields and wide-open meadows surrounded their path. Sunshine emitted from a brilliant sun and enhanced the countryside with everything its light had gently touched. Once the main road was a great distance behind them, Dani brought the car to a stop near a welcoming tree.

Samantha helped Dani unpack the car and settled in a nice, shaded area. Dominic jumped out of the back seat and shouted "Whoopee!" as he sprinted across the tall grassy fields. He held a kite up in the air with his right arm stretched as high as he could and ran in large circles. Samantha was delighted by her little boy's sense of innocence and playful joy. She caught herself in a stare while holding a picnic basket, her eyes fixed on Dominic. An overwhelming sense of emotion welled up.

"You alright?" Dani asked with concern.

Samantha broke loose of her trance and smiled abruptly to assure her friend that she was fine.

"Yeah. I'm fine."

She set down the basket filled with lunch and snacks on an unfolded multi-colored blanket and quickly wiped her face with both of her hands.

"You know, I thought this would be a wonderful place to enjoy for the afternoon. I'm so glad all of us are here together."

Dani's words were soothing. Samantha walked over to her best friend and hugged her.

"Thanks, Dani. I don't think I'd be able to handle this without you," Samantha replied with new tears streaming down a broken face. "It hurts that I won't be able to see him grow up and become the man that I see in him. And to know that at some point soon he'll see me fighting a terrible illness. That part crushes me."

They held each other beneath the warmth of the sun. A gentle breeze flowed around their picnic site and it reminded them both of how precious these moments became. As if the wind brought a sense of calm to ease any fear. But it was a new fear that began to stir in Samantha's center of her heart.

In the distance, Dominic laughed with a child's happiness and cheer as he ran through the open fields holding up his air glider in the wind. He was only a child, but his heart was equipped with the capacity to care for and to love others deeply. An attribute he received from his mother.

After a few hours, they relaxed after a satisfying meal. The day was just as she expected it would be. It was a peaceful getaway from the homestead, enjoying the company of Dani's friendship, and delighting in Dominic's untamed whimsy and playful joy. Then she realized she had forgotten to retrieve the box from the trunk. Before they left her home, she felt compelled to bring the dead crow's coffin along and bury it somewhere out in the country. It just seemed like the right thing to do.

"Did I bring the shovel?" Samantha asked as she stood and walked over to the car.

"Yeah, I saw it back there," said Dani, a bit puzzled. "I didn't ask, but I will now. Why on earth did you bring a shovel?"

"Well, I brought the box Mr. Harshom delivered last week," Samantha explained as she leaned over to pick up the crow's coffin and the shovel. "You remember, right?"

"Oh, how could I forget that thing?" Dani asked with a frown.

"I knew I had to give it a proper burial," said Samantha.

"Let me see it again."

Dani rushed over to take a closer look.

"Interesting box, but your name hand-painted on it is too much. Yeah, that's strange. The detail and care someone made for a dead bird. I don't get it. Was it his pet?" Dani chuckled to break the tense moment.

The mood suddenly became solemn as they both realized the depth of its meaning. They both stood quietly at the small coffin until Dominic's voice broke the silence.

"Hey, Mom! Whatcha doing?" Dominic ran over from a pile of sticks he collected and began constructing a small fort several yards away.

"Nothing, Dommie. Just talking about burying this box," she explained as she held it lower for him to see.

Dominic stood there puzzled for a few moments as he glanced at his mother's name and the number "32" painted on the surface. He quickly made a connection between his mother's wish transfer and this coffin.

"What's inside?" he asked.

"Well, a dead crow," she said. "It was a part of my wish transfer for you."

"Poor bird," he said, then leaned closer to the box and whispered, "Thank you."

Dominic jolted back to his stick creation.

Samantha placed the box on the ground and held the shovel securely. The grassy field made for a strenuous dig, but she was persistent and formed a hole deep enough to fit the coffin. After a pile of fresh soil mixed with a top layer of grass was neatly compiled, she laid the tool down and wiped her head. The heat of the afternoon wasn't a burden during the activity, but she felt winded and warm to the touch. The dig took no more than several minutes. Yet she felt strangely fatigued for such a brief activity.

Her mind shifted to the ceremonial drink and her wish. *Could it be so soon* she thought? *Is the illness already making its way through my body?* She usually kept physically fit and had no problems tending to her garden or other yard work. This was concerning.

"Hey, Mom!" blurted Dominic and broke her thoughts. "Look behind you. Birds!"

"What?" she answered as she turned to see what he was referring to.

Standing in the grassy fields, about twenty-five yards away, watched a large group of crows. They were silent and didn't announce their arrival. Dani and Samantha were surprised to see them. Probably because they heard no sounds at all. Typically, birds will flutter their wings as they land and crows will caw loudly. But not this time.

"What is going on?"

Dani spoke slowly as she stared at the group of crows that stared right back at them.

"I'm freaking out. Is this some kind of funeral gathering?"

"Not sure," Samantha replied in a mild shock and somewhat dazed. She shook off her stare.

"I've got to finish."

"What about these crows?" Dani pointed to them and looked towards Samantha.

"Just ignore them. I'm sure they'll fly away in a few minutes."

Samantha kneeled to inspect the hole; to be sure the box would fit and brushed away at the edges breaking loose more dirt. She scooped out a little more with her hands and leaned over to grab the box. Then, a crow shrieked and the cluster of birds flew near the burial site in a matter of seconds. They encircled the hole within a few feet. She stopped and was frightened by their furtive movement.

"Are you behind me?" Samantha asked nervously.

"Yeah. I'm right here," Dani said in a weird tone. "This is scaring me."

"I know. Me too, but just remain calm and stay close," Samantha was now reassuring in her voice. "Just take the shovel and hold it, just in case."

Dani slowly bent down to take the shovel and she huddled behind her friend in a catcher's stance. Samantha took her eyes off the clan of crows and continued to move the coffin into the burial hole carefully. The crows didn't make a sound. Their eyes were fixed on her actions and concentrated on her movements. Once it was placed down in its resting position, she grabbed the pile of soil and chunks of grass with both hands. Heaps of earth were dropped onto the box until the hole was filled.

"Now what?" Dani said.

"Let's wait. Just a moment," Samantha whispered.

"You have to say something." Dominic interrupted, as he continued to play. "Just like they did when Daddy died."

She turned her head towards Dominic, surprised he would say such a thing. He continued to play with the sticks quietly and he was unfazed by the crows. Almost as if he was familiar with them; as if he knew they would be there. The concern showed in her frown. Those words bothered her and were a reminder of her husband's presence she no longer felt.

"Alright, Dommie," she agreed. Samantha looked down at the mound she formed and began to speak.

"Life is precious, life is sweet, and it is a wonder. But even the best of our years are filled with pain and heartache. Soon those years will disappear and we fly away."

The moment was tense with these strange guests and their eerie behavior. Still, this seemed like the proper thing to do. Samantha stood motionless as she stared at the group of crows. They did nothing for several moments and then suddenly one broke their silence with annoying, ear-piercing shrieks. The noise startled Dani and Samantha, but their curiosity prevented them from chasing them away.

The act was one of ultimate respect for their fallen comrade. Sure, to everyone who lived in this land they were nothing more than crows. But to their kind, a unique clan of sacred protectors of something greater than themselves. They are elite guardians and faithful ambassadors of the wish transfer.

The one who appeared to be their leader was larger and more assertive than the rest. It let out a loud, unique cry and the women covered their ears from its unnerving sound. Dominic continued to play, undistracted. Then the leader lifted itself into the air with its wings in motion and hovered over the burial for several seconds. Samantha and Dani watched with caution and they were ready for a possible attack. The intimidating crow quickly elevated up into the sky directly above where it once hovered and the rest of the birds dashed upwards into the air and followed behind. They were visible only for a few moments, then they slowly disappeared through the clouds as they ascended swiftly.

"Okay, that was nuts!" said Dani amazed.

"Yeah. Something you'd see in a movie, right?" said Samantha. "I guess it was some sort of way they pay their respects to their own."

~

The drive home was longer than expected. Perhaps it was the awkwardness of what had transpired with the burial and the heaviness on their hearts that made it so, but their escape into the country made for an exhausted little boy. Dominic was now in dreamland as he was safely strapped into his seat.

For him, the trip was enlightening and playful. He was drawn to vast open spaces with rolling hills and sensational views. His sense of imagination was delighted by such splendor. As if he belonged there; a beckoning from the outer reaches of Esid Arapym.

As Dominic slept, his mind wandered into a realm of fantastic wonder. A place with vibrant colors not seen anywhere in the world. A magnificent place where imagination meets the afterlife. The glory that surrounded him felt warm and homelike. Gladness and joyfulness abounded there without dread or helplessness. He began to sprint through numerous gardens that were never-ending. One by one, he flashed by fields with swaying flowers and the greenest herbage. With his arms outstretched he laughed wildly without purpose; the happiness sprung from deep within his heart.

In the distance, he saw a figure of someone he faintly recognized. He continued running, but now towards this person. It resembled his father, Russell, but he wasn't quite sure. His heart pounded, not from the rapid speed of his flight on foot, but from the anticipation of what he hoped this man could be. Dominic ran closer. He could now make out the details of this person's face. It couldn't be. As he reached him, it was unmistakable—he was his father. Dominic leaped into Russell's open arms and they embraced as the skies greeted them with applause.

"Daddy!" Dominic shouted with glee. "It's you! It's you!"

Dominic's heart was overwhelmed with sensations of pure bliss. There was nowhere or nothing else he imagined could be better than this moment.

"I've missed you so much," Russell said as he held his son and swayed from side to side. They both shed tears of perfect joy.

"I miss you, Daddy," his son answered. "I don't want to let you go."

They looked into each other's eyes and began walking through picturesque scenes of intense beauty. Russell held Dominic's hand and they spent hours talking about a great many things. He told his father stories about what had happened after he had passed on; how his heart was broken, but also how he must be a grown-up to take care of his mother. Russell was so proud of his boy and he told him so. He also encouraged Dominic to continue his life with purpose, with passion, and forever keep loving others. A father's love never ends and this same love even lives and breathes within a child's dreams.

After what seemed like an entire day, Russell told his son that he had to leave. Dominic wasn't sad, though. He knew this meeting with his father was special and he could see him again when he dreamed. They embraced one final time and Russell smiled with great admiration.

"I'll see you again, Dommie."

Russell waved as he walked away and disappeared into the deepest violet sky.

"Goodbye, Daddy!" Dominic stood waving back at his father.

Dani pulled the car into Samantha's driveway and turned it off. Dominic felt the engine's motion stop and it caused him to escape from his sleep. He forced open his tired eyes and looked over at his house.

"Hey, kiddo. We're home," Samantha said. "How was your nap?"

He wiped his eyes with his curled-up fingers and yawned. Dominic looked satisfied and relieved.

"It was a good dream."

Samantha opened the car door and stepped out. She pulled their picnic belongings out of the car with Dani's help.

"Yeah, I'm beat," said Dani as she yawned.

"Hey, thanks for driving," said Samantha. "We had a great time."

"Not a problem," said Dani. "We need more of these getaways."

Later that evening, as Samantha tucked Dominic into his covers, he thanked her for being such a good mother to him. The unexpected words surprised her, and she looked into his loving eyes.

"You're welcome. I love you so much and nothing will ever change that."

Her voice trembled slightly with emotion.

"I know these days have been so hard on you ever since Daddy's been gone."

"But I saw him in my dream today," he said eagerly as his face lit up and he sat upright.

"Oh, that's wonderful," she said with eyes that longed to see Russell.

"Don't be sad. He's in a good place," he said with excitement. "So many colors in the sky and he hugged me."

She pulled him closer and hugged Dominic as she let out her uncontrollable sobbing. Her son's embrace meant everything to her. She could not contain every ounce of grief and love at that moment. It broke through the seams of her heart because she knew her time was short. But little did she know that it was shorter than she anticipated.

CHAPTER 6

Beneath a glorious spray of a new day's fresh sunshine, he appeared among the tranquil landscape. An uninvited guest's invasion of a spectacular day was felt by every living thing. His presence was thick and his aroma was death itself. He persuaded the weak and preyed upon the hopeless. But the beauty that surrounded him would not surrender their position, their display of glory and pride. No, not here at this place of peace and power.

Clyde Serwhoven confidently approached the powerful tree with poise. With each step closer to his destination, the alerted crows became a barrier between him and Mara. A great many of them flew from the crow's den to mount a defense. It was a massive campaign with what appeared to be dozens of crows. Each one stood its ground primed for an attack; their beaks ready to taste his defeat and their iron-like talons capable to shred his flesh with swift fury.

"I see you keep your pets well trained," Clyde said to Mara.

He stopped and stood nearly forty feet away from its mammoth trunk and the crows formed a line halfway between them.

"But, they are merely fowl."

He looked at them with disgust in his eyes. Clyde summed up his opposition as he glanced from left to right.

Mara towered over him with powerful outstretched limbs that spread in every direction. Its shade blocked the morning sunlight from his piercing eyes. There was silence for a few moments, then the tree's inaudible response was heard in his head.

"What is the purpose of your visit, Clyde? I don't remember inviting you," said Mara.

"No need for an invitation. I do whatever I please. I thought you would know that by now," he said with a smirk. "I've come to warn you concerning your feeble cause. Your insignificant and hopeless chore of aiding those in Esid Arapym is going to reduce your existence to dust. That is my promise to you."

Mara's reply was felt throughout his bones.

"You have no power here and your pitiful threats are meaningless. Your agenda has no bearing on what I will continue to accomplish. A few faithful are all that I require. For as long as I live, there will be life in others. And I will not perish."

He shuddered at her words. Then continued to speak sternly without making eye contact with the tree.

"Well, you only have so many remaining birdies. To my understanding, thirty-two crows have been sacrificed for previous wishes. And I figure you require many more to mount an appropriate resistance against my onslaught."

Clyde assumed that his nemesis, Mara, could not counter the number of stricken people infected by Stillwhorm Syndrome. He considered this an early victory over Mara, because of how many crows would be required to die for wish transfers. But he assumed far too much.

He waited then turned his eyes upward to Mara's towering expanse.

"Oh, you mean the widow and her boy? I would dismiss your faith in her decision to carry her wish over to her child. She is a wounded and helpless mass of flesh with nothing but grief at her core. And as you are well aware, she is already doomed by her decision," he said and grinned sharply. "My mission will be completed.

The sinister figure believed with everything that he held a vital position against the people and against all that Mara stood for. His bitter interest fueled his passionate hate for the good within the tree. His belief in his power was enhanced to new levels with each victim who died from the illness. He was proud of the deadly blow he delivered. But, sometimes his dark pride clouded his view.

Although, his fierce anger burned brightly towards Samantha—a rage that was sparked long ago. Clyde remembered how her parents declared on the day of her birth that she would be a significant person in the land and how through her life she would deliver a blow to illness itself. That because of Samantha, one day a powerful flow of healing would revive the residents of Esid Arapym. Specifically, Stillwhorm Syndrome would be eradicated.

Now, just because two parents have spoken goodness into their child does not mean it would come to pass. But, they were not merely parents or typical people. No, they were both gifted with a unique calling in their lives. From as early as they could remember, they spoke words of great power and the essence of goodness flowed through what they declared verbally. Outcomes leaned in favor of their declarations. Some refer to those with this calling as *Petitioners*.

Clyde realized their ability and he was familiar with their kind; their words carried tremendous strength. It would be his pursuit to stop the flow of cleansing the land through their daughter as they had declared, somehow. Yet, all through her life, she was guarded by her Petitioner's words and she became untouchable. He lurked around every corner in an attempt to plot a way to infect her, to no avail. Until the day she opened herself up to the deadly sting of Stillwhorm by the hand of her own decision. Her wish transfer.

A chilling delirium rose from his spine as Clyde took two more steps toward Mara and immediately the crow named Chancellor swiftly descended from within the tree. He suddenly paused as Chancellor challenged Clyde and hovered in flight directly across from his eyes in attack formation, but out of arm's reach. Its wings flapped almost in slow motion because their span was remarkable and they had such powerful strokes. This epic crow was the fiercest of the guardians and it was ready to take Clyde down.

He clenched both fists ready to engage, but something abruptly caught his attention elsewhere. Something vital from somewhere else in Esid Arapym. His head turned to look behind him over his shoulder, then he looked back at Mara with an evil glare in his stale eyes.

"Do you hear that? Duty calls. I have an immediate engagement that requires my personal touch," he said. "It is Samantha's time and I've waited years for this. There is nothing purer and more satisfying than divine destiny. Good day."

He sensed that particular moment in her body when the dormant illness—mysteriously infused into her from her wish transfer—was now ready to manifest and consume her. Only Clyde could perceive this within these victims. Only he could commence the ravage by Stillworm Syndrome.

Clyde then turned and disappeared into the landscape.

The crows resumed their places on the tree, but Chancellor flew upward high enough for a broad view to be certain the sinister one did not have a change of heart and return. Once he faded from view, the leader of the crows returned to its high position on Mara.

Clyde rarely made his appearance at this place of solitude. But Mara did not feel threatened. His visit only revealed the lack of conviction in himself. It was the first time he felt threatened by the promise—the covenant Mara established with those in Esid Arapym long ago. The tree's existence was their only hope for those who were willing to sacrifice themselves for others. And that empowerment recently placed in the hands of Samantha was the beginning of Clyde's diminishing confidence in his mission. And her threat also stoked the fire that raged inside of him and his poisonous sting. He purposed more than ever to crush Samantha and her child.

~

A gloominess filled the room from the absence of light, blocked by the closed drapes. Silence permeated the air except for the faint sounds of a mother's steady breathing. Samantha slept peacefully and entertained a collection of lofty dreams. Her bedroom was still and quiet. Yet, a chilling presence stood in the opposite corner of her room.

Clyde seeped through the impenetrable walls of the Parsons' home. Like vapors moving through a shield made with fibrous mesh; his skill overpowered the laws of physics. It was his moment, the one he had been waiting for. He finally reached the onset of her doom. With deep intentional breaths, Clyde patiently embraced the moment as he trained his piercing eyes upon his perfect victim.

He slowly approached the foot of Samantha's bed just as a stalking predator calculates its movement. Clyde pushed his head forward over his shoulders to smell any of her silent fear and he stopped just inches away from the edge of her bed. After a pause, he leaned down, reached out with his index finger, and brought it to her blanket that covered her legs. It was time to trigger the onset of Stillwhorm Syndrome and begin her demise.

With ease, his finger touched the fabric of her coverings and penetrated through until his skin met with her ankle. The slightest prod was all that he needed to complete his task. It was so slight it did not awaken her. Within that graze of her skin and his an immediate flow began to her bloodstream. Cells carried his poison into her vascular system and invaded her body. He smiled with the deepest gratification he ever had.

Clyde removed his finger from her ankle and out through the blankets without any evidence of a tear or hole in the fabric. He stood upright and gazed at her. Samantha now turned over in her bed as if something unsettled her once peaceful sleep pattern. The slightest agitation from this evil sent signals throughout her body and caused her restless sleep for the remaining few hours.

Now completely and thoroughly satisfied, Clyde turned and walked out of her room and down the hallway in eerie silence. After a few steps, he stopped when he was outside Dominic's room. The closed-door prevented him from looking at the boy and he knew there was no way to bring harm to him. The power of his mother's wish transfer was far superior to even Clyde's arsenal. Dominic was sealed with the love of Samantha's act and the promise of Mara's goodness.

Clyde sneered and continued walking down the hall and towards the front door. He contained the heart of terror, just as a night stalker would leave out of the front door of a victim's dwelling after committing a hideous act. Pride and arrogance enveloped Clyde's existence.

He vanished out into the mist that covered the front lawn long before a new day rose.

The sunrise peered through her drapes and gently nudged Samantha's eyelids. She slowly opened her eyes and frowned at the early daylight that found her. The slight separation in the drapery allowed this calm awakening, but it was unwanted.

Her hands reached for her head and she held it carefully. Her finger's light touch against her temples delivered jabs of ache. It was the dull pain directly behind her eyes that crept over the top of her forehead that made her long for more sleep. But the throbbing demanded to be dealt with and forced her out of her warm bed.

She let out a slight moan as she sat upright on the edge of the mattress. Her right hand still gently touching her forehead, she stood and slowly approached her bathroom. After switching on the bright vanity light, she immediately turned it off because the brightness aggravated her pain. Her eyes glanced up to the mirror and her reflection was not pleasing at all. A paleness stood there in the place where she once recognized her beautiful skin. Bloodshot eyes and dry lips also covered her facial expression. Samantha was concerned and her mind raced back to her birthday, to her wish transfer. *Was this the beginning of my end?* She paused for a moment and was in a mild state of shock.

It had only been a brief two-week period since her birthday. Although she was fully aware of the consequential decision she made for her precious Dominic, she hoped that this day would somehow be delayed for a season or much longer. Perhaps never occur at all. Samantha began to panic and sob uncontrollably. She held her hands pressed against her eyes as if she was pushing back against this dread. It was useless. Stillwhorm was fierce and showed no mercy to any of its victims. It would take every morsel of strength within her to fight this certain spell of doom. She would need her strength to stay alive for as long as she could. Stay alive for her son.

Twenty minutes later, Dominic woke from his peaceful night of rest. He turned his head towards the door of his bedroom because he sensed someone was there. Samantha stood there motionless and leaned against the doorframe with her arms to her side.

"Morning."

Dominic greeted his mother as he wiped the sleepiness from his eyes.

"Why are you standing there?"

He was a bit confused by her blank stare. Normally she would tip-toe through his room to wake him with a kiss, but this time she didn't act the same. No, this morning brought a devastating blow to her health.

"Good morning. I was just about to wake you, but I was caught up in the moment. And I'm not feeling too well."

She walked over to his bed and sat next to him. Her fingers pushed his bangs to the side and she leaned over and kissed his forehead. How many more of these moments would she have?

"I'm hungry," he blurted out with a yawn. "Can you please make me my favorite?"

It was obvious to her and the rest of the world that his favorite meant wild berry hotcakes with sweet fruit topping. Because that was a mouthful to say so early in the morning, he chose to refer to it as favorite—nothing more.

Samantha chuckled because of his cuteness and his innocence. It was her honor to prepare anything he asked for to eat. She delighted in every single moment with him.

"Of course. Coming right up."

She smiled with a deep appreciation for this moment.

"Now you jump out of bed and get yourself ready for the day while I go slave in the kitchen for you," she said with a frown and in her deepest voice she could find.

Thirty-three Crows

He laughed from deep in his belly. He appreciated her humor and her lightheartedness with things. He gladly went along with her make-believe and it made his heart very happy.

"You're funny," he said.

And so the day began with a sudden dose of reality for Samantha. The call of the sacred drink summoned her to inevitable fate. It was the beginning of her end. Her life would soon come crashing down like a wall of autumn leaves toppled by a violent wind. Yes, the day was marked for her death as the countdown began. Only, there was no telling how many days she had before she took her last breath.

~

Dani rushed in through the front door and hurried into the living room. She gasped and had a look of concern as she raced to Samantha's lifeless body. Dominic was kneeling by her side still holding the telephone in his hand. He called Dani immediately after his mother had collapsed.

"Sam! Samantha!"

Dani gently tapped her friend's cheek with an open hand as she urgently called her name repeatedly. Samantha had a pulse and was breathing, but she was unresponsive.

"Sam! Can you hear me? Wake up!"

Dani grabbed the phone from Dominic and began to dial for help.

Dominic cried holding his mother's hand to his chest. His shoulders caved with each crying breath. His mind raced to the events of the recent past when his father became ill. Moments of his father lying in the hospital bed, suffering, overwhelmed his heart. It was too much for a little boy to endure. Too much for anyone to endure, for that matter.

As Dani spoke quickly to the authorities, she reached out her arm to hold Dominic. She whispered to him between her conversations with the operator.

"It's going to be alright, Dommie. I'm here."

Dominic nodded his head as he continued to rub Samantha's hand across his cheek wet with tears.

The scene played out as an emergency medical aid response should. Vehicles and personnel cluttering the living room once peaceful and tranquil. Before calamity struck. Before Samantha toppled to the carpet.

As Dani held onto Dominic and comforted him, the medical team prepared Samantha for a trip to the hospital. They moved with purpose and discipline as all hands moved in unison to care for her. A paramedic asked Dani some questions and wrote her responses down on a large clipboard. The flashing red lights from emergency vehicles shone through the windows and lit up the living room with blazes of intense crimson. They danced upon the walls like flames on an open campfire.

Minutes later, Samantha's eyes finally opened, but they were now capturing images of stainless steel directly above her. Medical equipment and a gloved person in uniform hovered over her head. She realized based on her surroundings that she was in an ambulance. Loud wailing sirens and every so often an annoying pump of the horn added to her sensory perception. But she was still foggy and dazed, unaware of how this moment even began. She focused on every detail around her to account for this reality.

"Samantha? Can you hear me?" the calm voice of the gloved man in uniform broke her concentration. "Samantha Parsons?"

"Ye…yes. I can."

The ambulance medic could barely understand her words.

"Okay. You're going to be alright. We're taking you to the ER now," he said while taking her blood pressure on her right arm.

"Huh?"

Samantha squinted her eyes trying to focus on his face. Her vision was still blurry.

"ER?" she asked in confusion.

"You passed out. You'll be fine," he reassured her. "We're almost there."

The ambulance drove through the last intersection before it slowed and turned into the hospital driveway. After a pause and into a reverse motion, the vehicle came to a stop at the curbside of S. Childs Memorial Emergency Department. The rear doors opened and in a smooth motion, the team had her securely on the gurney being wheeled through the emergency entrance. Dani and Dominic followed in her car as closely as possible and parked in the visitor's area. She held his hand as they hurried through the parking lot and approached the main entrance.

After the medical staff began their initial assessment and drew her blood for tests, the team left her alone to rest. She was safe from harm's way and she was stable. The last nurse pulled the curtain around her bed to give her some privacy. Samantha felt numb from her fall and she began collecting her thoughts. One by one, she replayed in her mind what she was doing leading up to the ambulance ride. She remembered Dominic's face as she was preparing breakfast. Then, she recalled him helping her with the dishes. And walking from the kitchen to her room was all she could remember.

The curtain was pulled back and a man greeted her. He introduced himself as Dr. Michael Brimmer. He wore a dress shirt and a tie and emitted a sense of calmness through his eyes. His trimmed beard reminded her of Russell.

"It's nice to meet you, Samantha. I'm sorry it's under these terrible conditions."

He was soft-spoken and caring. Somehow, she knew he was a gentle person who had a depth to his character. It was strange to her that she sensed so much about him after a brief encounter.

"Where's my son?" she asked.

Those were her first words out of her mouth. Her greatest concern was not her condition or her manners, but it was solely for Dominic.

"Your son is in the waiting room with your friend. He was shaken up a bit but doing better now."

He slid a chair close to her side and sat down.

"You don't mind if I sit here while we chat, do you?"

"No."

Samantha's eyes drifted away towards the pale-yellow wall brightly lit by recessed lighting in the high ceiling tiles. She didn't want to believe the news she was about to hear.

Dr. Brimmer placed her chart down on the table beside her bed and turned to her eyes.

"I know how much this hurts right now," he said.

"You have no idea, doctor," she answered without hesitation and kept staring away from him. "You have no idea how much this hurts my heart."

Her tears began to fall and her hands were shaking as she lifted them to wipe her face.

"I already know what you're about to say. I know what I have."

Dr. Brimmer's face changed. It was once kind a few moments ago, but now it suddenly became transformed into grief. Stone-like and with pursed lips, he answered quietly.

"I lost my wife four years ago to Stillwhorm. And it crushed me."

Samantha turned to face him. She rested her hands over her chest, clenching the top of the thin blanket with her fists.

"I'm sorry, doctor. I lost my husband almost a year ago."

Her tears broke through her speech and her chin trembled.

"I'm terribly sorry," Dr. Brimmer consoled her as best he could. "My words can do very little, but we are going to do everything we can to help you through this time."

He smiled and held out his hand to hold hers. She smiled back and nodded her head.

"I'm going to fight this for as long as I can for my son," she said.

"I understand you gave your son, Dominic, the best gift you could have ever given him," he said. "A wish transfer is something we don't hear about these days. And you made a brave decision to protect him. I'm very proud of you, Samantha."

He continued to grin with a peaceful look in his eyes. Samantha smiled and appreciated his kind demeanor.

"It was all I could do to protect him and guard him against this terrible illness. May I see him now?" she asked.

"Absolutely. I'll get him and your friend."

Dr. Brimmer stood and turned to her before leaving.

"We're going to keep you overnight to determine if there is anything else going on in your body. This will allow us to have your port placed in your upper chest for future infusions. So, we'll get that done as well. Otherwise, if you are clear and feeling better, we'll discharge you tomorrow."

"Thank you," she said.

Samantha felt a bit of relief knowing she could return home and make more beautiful memories with Dominic. Before things got worse. Before the sinister disease consumed her.

When the doctor left the room Samantha heard eerie silence in the room. It was overwhelming. The solitude, even though it lasted for a couple of minutes, assaulted her mind with her looming defeat. She thought it was strange that she could almost hear faint whispers in her mind. Spoken words from the lips of evil itself. And these words sounded like they came from Clyde Serwhoven. She tried to push these thoughts out, but they consumed her and assaulted her heart.

She glanced around the room to be sure he wasn't there or standing outside in the hallway. No one was there. Just her thoughts drowning in the solitary moment. She became scared like no other time in her life. The type of fright that sends shivers through the spine.

CHAPTER 7

The small iron kettle was carefully placed on a woven place setting in the center of his mother's favorite chestnut tray. They were both family heirlooms passed down from previous generations and held tremendous value. Samantha's mug, a silver spoon, and a fancy folded napkin accompanied honey and a smooth fresh-herb tea bag. A unique hand-picked bouquet from the garden was proudly set alongside the kettle by Dominic. Dani spread these elements evenly on the tray and asked Dominic to deliver them to his mother who was resting in her bedroom.

He picked up the tray with both hands as if his life depended upon it. There would be no spilling of the tea this afternoon. He balanced his movement, each step taken with caution, as his eyes aimed for his mother's room.

"Mommy, I'm on my way to your room now," announced Dominic.

His voice was sure and confident.

Samantha rested in her soft leather chair near her bedroom window. She was covered in a quilt and focused on the ballet of leaves falling outside beyond her window. Her thoughts swept her away into melancholy. But, when she heard his voice, she adjusted her countenance from sullen to grateful and bright in preparation for Dominic's arrival.

As Dominic entered her bedroom, he previewed the landing spot with studying eyes for his delivery of teatime. An empty, tall table was available right next to Samantha's chair. His slow movement was adorable in the sight of his mother. She leaned over her chair's armrest to offer assistance, but he nodded in disagreement.

"I can do it. I'm a big boy now," he reassured Samantha.

Since her sudden illness episode a few days ago Dominic felt compelled to take up more responsibility with her care and with the household duties. He also believed that the wish transfer imputed a sense of maturity to him and he was not about to waste that special gift.

"Thank you, sweetie," Samantha replied as she poured herself a cup of tea.

Dominic looked at her with satisfaction. Her first sip brought warmth to her, extending down to her feet. Her body, now invaded by Stillwhorm, felt cold most of the day. The simple goodness of hot tea was something she did not take for granted.

"It's sensational. Thank you for taking such good care of me."

Dominic grinned sheepishly and ran off to find some big adventure outside. He was affected emotionally by his mother's condition but used every opportunity he could to remain a child. His imagination ran wild and he used this ability to escape for brief moments while he played with his toys. His mother's garden was one of his favorite spots at their home. It was a haven for him, so he felt. And occasionally he noticed a bird perched upon a tree limb nearby. It was a very attentive crow.

Later that same afternoon, it was time for Samantha's treatment. She gathered a few things of personal belongings in a floral design tote and made sure Dominic was ready. She drove to the medical facility allocated only for Stillwhorm Syndrome care. It was a large facility with many floors and about a fifteen-minute drive from their home. Dominic brought a favorite toy with him to keep himself occupied.

After settling into the treatment room, a dedicated personal space with a bed and a few chairs, she was met by Dr. Brimmer. His voice was cheery.

"Hello, Samantha. How are you feeling today?"

"I have chills running throughout my body nearly all of the time," she replied.

"Okay. Unfortunately, this is one of the early-stage symptoms you'll be facing."

He reviewed her chart for a moment then quickly looked over at Dominic who sat in a chair. The doctor had a nice rapport with patients and their family members.

"Hello, Dominic. How are you?"

"Pretty good," he answered confidently.

The doctor was amused by his charm, then he turned back to his patient.

"Now Samantha, your vitals are holding nicely right where they need to be. This is wonderful. As you and I had discussed earlier in the week, you will receive three to four infusions weekly for approximately three weeks. We would like to see the SS levels—a term we use for Stillwhorm Syndrome—remain at a minimum level for as long as we can. The treatments may be arduous but prove to be rather effective."

She turned to look at Dominic for a few seconds then back to Dr. Brimmer.

"Yes, I fully understand the course of care. Let's get started."

"Very good," he replied. "Then I'll let you get set up by your nurse. Please ask me if you need anything. I'll be around."

"I will. Thanks again," Samantha said.

Dr. Brimmer walked out just as Mary walked in with an infusion bag. It was a combination of two medicines used in the early stages of the illness. She greeted Samantha and Dominic while she hung the bag to prep the intravenous fluid with the plastic tubing. Mary was a very kind nurse who had been in the unit for many years.

Samantha chose to lay on the bed while she listened to music that played from the room's television. Soothing and peaceful melodies eased her tension during the lengthy treatment. The infusion was administered through her new intravenous port near her left collar bone, which was implanted during her initial visit. A very sharp needle on the end of the tubing punctured her skin once it was sanitized. After a brief pinch, the nurse adjusted the settings on the medical pump and began the run of medicine. Samantha let out a long exhale and closed her eyes.

Mary walked over to Dominic and checked on him. She asked if he would like a coloring book and markers. He happily said yes and prepared himself and area at the table in the corner. She brought him a variety of supplies and two books for him to enjoy. He had a composure that was years beyond his young age and a level of patience to match.

After an hour of her infusion, the medical pump began to chirp a low-sounding beep. It was time to hang a new bag. A typical course required three bags.

Dominic whispered as he splashed forest green within dark outlines on the page, still focused on his task.

"Bag change."

Mary returned holding a new bag and placed it at the top of the IV pole. As Samantha remained still with her eyes closed covered by a warm blanket, the nurse changed bags and resumed the pump.

"How are you doing, Samantha?" Mary asked quietly.

"I'm fine," she replied. "Just wiped out and feeling exhausted."

"Would you like anything to drink or eat?" she asked.

"No, thanks. Maybe in a while."

Mary walked out and the second wave of infusion therapy moved throughout her body. Outside of her room in the hallway, a small group of people approached the main desk. They were a young group in their thirties. One man began talking with the charge nurse. They held large bags filled with hand-sewn quilts and beanie caps. After a few minutes, the group walked down the halls going from room to room as directed by the nursing staff. They made sure the patients they visited were feeling up to visitation.

Once the third bag was hung and it was now in Samantha's third hour of treatment, she asked her nurse for a hot cup of tea and a sandwich. Then, after asking Dominic, she also asked her to bring him a kid's meal as well. Although the treatment was exhausting to her body, she would feel better with a light meal towards the last phase of the infusions. Samantha paid close attention to her body during the course of care so that she could make good use of her time. When she felt well, she made sure to engage with her boy and those around her. It was her way of empowerment during her crisis.

As she and Dominic enjoyed their meal together in the treatment room, Mary came in to check on them.

"Are you up for a short visit by some guests, Samantha?" her nurse asked. "A team of volunteers comes by frequently to offer blankets to our patients. Since you're up and eating, I thought you might like a visit."

"Sure. That sounds nice," Samantha said as she wiped her mouth with a napkin. "I could use some uplifting interaction."

"Okay. I'll let them know," Mary replied and walked out.

She knew that Dani would not always be able to join her during her infusion appointments, so anyone she could get to know during her ongoing care would be beneficial. And Samantha was a social person without the need to feel too private concerning her medical plight. She invited friends into her life, especially after the loss of her husband.

There was a gentle knock at the door and a voice on the other side.

"Hello."

Samantha put down her cup of tea and answered.

"Come in."

The door opened slowly as a kind-faced man peeked around it. He was with two others, a couple, both holding large tote bags. He introduced himself and his companions to Samantha.

"Good afternoon. My name is Julius and this is Naomi and Frank. We're with the Compassion United Organization and we'd like to offer you a beanie and a quilt."

His voice cut through the stale hospital room silence with a sense of calmness. They approached Samantha as she sat upright in her bed.

"Hello. I'm Samantha and this is my son, Dominic. It's very nice to meet you all."

Dominic stood and greeted the team.

"Hi. Would you like to color with me?" he asked them.

Naomi walked over to the table to join him.

"I sure would," she said as she pulled up a chair next to him.

Julius stood like a tall, peaceful figure in the room. It was his amazing smile and his kind face that struck Samantha. Julius and Frank walked over to her and offered their gifts.

"Please pick your favorite color. We understand that this is a difficult time for you. You might benefit from something warm," Julius said.

"I need some warmth in life right about now," she answered. "This is so wonderful. What is the Compassion United Organization? I've not heard of them."

"We're an organization that offers a compassionate gesture to those who are fighting any illness or disease. I'm surprised you haven't heard of us. We've been offering our little bit of hope for quite some time now."

Julius retrieved his wallet and handed her a business card with his number on it.

"If you need anything, just give me a call. I'm the unofficial director of services."

Naomi chimed in from her coloring time with Dominic.

"Come on, Julius. You can't always be so humble. Samantha, this is our fearless leader, point man, and OFFICIAL director," she touted. "He doesn't like to share some of his accolades. And he also is the founder of our organization. We refer to it as CU. He's been doing this for nearly three years."

"Wow," Samantha said. "I'm impressed."

She accepted his card and began sorting through the collection of quilts.

"Please don't be," Julius answered. "I just want to help others. It's my purpose in life, my calling."

He smiled and put his arm around Frank.

"We do this together. Right, Frank?"

"Absolutely," Frank said. "We like to think of ourselves as thankful people serving others in crisis."

"Well, I need some of what you're offering during this crazy time. I just began my first treatment for Stillwhorm and I'll need any support I can get," Samantha said. "I lost my husband almost a year ago and now it's just me and Dominic."

She continued after holding back her tears.

"This is the hardest time of my life and I need to be the strongest I can for my son. I don't have any other family, but I do have a best friend who always helps. Her name is Dani and she's a wonderful person. Sort of like you are, Julius."

He looked down for a moment then glanced at Dominic.

"Thank you. I'm sure your friend is very special. And I'm sorry to hear about your husband. You have our deepest sympathies," said Julius. His words were like a salve to her ache.

She paused for a moment, then resumed her selection.

"I love your assortment of quilts. I just might choose this one with a colorful floral design. Thank you so much."

"It's our pleasure," said Julius.

"You're welcome," said Frank.

It was a victorious moment for a single mother facing a daunting crisis. The Compassion Team made their introduction and offered an additional layer of support in her world. The timing was essential because she felt her world crumbling, tearing at the seams from the onset of this deadliest disease known in this era. Without a cure and a sprinkle of any hope, Julius made his introduction at the perfect time.

She remained in bed for the duration of her infusion and her new friends said goodbye to Samantha and Dominic. Just as she had realized from her first earlier treatments, she had some lift in her spirit after her tea and sandwich. But this time it was a different sense of uplifting—not merely in her physical state, but also her heart. Could it be that Julius and his team made such an impact with one brief visit? Maybe, but she found a new enthusiasm to discover more with them and nothing would be able to separate her from her new friends. That's what hope does.

~

Thirty-three Crows

Two hours later, the Compassion United Team completed their rounds on the floor and said their goodbyes to the staff. They walked down the hallway and through the waiting room. Their smiles were infectious and each demeanor was upbeat. As they walked by the only person who sat there reading a magazine, Julius sensed something evil in that room. The reading material was lowered slightly to reveal the person's eyes watching the group walk by. It was Clyde. Nothing was said.

Julius, Naomi, and Frank walked through the rest of the facility and headed outside. Their conversation centered on their new friend they just met and her adorable son. It was another rewarding day for the team of hope givers.

Clyde sat there patiently while he held a magazine out in front of him. He decided to remain close by his victim at the medical center. He waited patiently in that stuffy room.

"I wonder how you're doing, Samantha?"

He muttered under his breath to himself.

"Time is not on your side. In fact, with every second that passes, you draw closer to your husband. Your dead husband."

He set down the magazine on the table in front of his chair and folded his leg over the other. Clyde was in no hurry.

CHAPTER 8

The rumble of children's voices filled the rooms for the first time since the school released them for their long break. They were restless and giddy among their peers. Dominic was one of the hundreds of other students waiting for the bell to commence the first day of school.

Samantha stood with the other parents outside of Dominic's classroom. They peered at their children through the large window in the door. Just minutes before, Samantha walked Dominic to his desk that had his name taped to the pencil box. She told him how much she loved him and how much she would miss him during the time he was at school.

The school bell rang throughout the campus and broke the energy in every room. Classes began for the children at Eden Peak Elementary School. And parents began to flood the exits in clusters and head back to their vehicles. Including Samantha, although she paused for a while longer as she admired her son from behind the closed classroom door. She had not been separated from him for this much time since Russell had passed. It will be difficult for her to adjust her days without having Dominic nearby. But she now had additional friends to lean on as well as Dani.

Her last treatment was administered the week before school began and she was strengthened by the course of the medicine. Dr. Brimmer excelled in his area of specialty—Stillwhorm Syndrome—and after only three weeks of treatment, her health improved. If at least she could buy herself more time with Dominic and Dani, then that would be terrific. Each day at this point was a gift and she did not take any of her breaths for granted.

Dr. Brimmer cautioned her to not overextend herself physically because of her weakened state, but she was cleared for most activities for the time being. She followed his strict course of diet, rest, and weekly appointments. The doctor monitored her condition closely. She was a star patient.

~

Julius welcomed Samantha as she walked into the coffee shop. She waved at him as she pointed to the counter and walked to the employee behind the register. Her latest beverage of choice was one of either two blends of local tea. She ordered a medium lemon-berry with a small amount of cream and joined Julius at his table by the window.

"Hi there," she said holding her steaming cup.

"Hello," he replied. "It's so nice to see you outside of the hospital. You feeling okay?"

Samantha took her first sip and smiled.

"Mmmm. This is wonderful. I'm feeling pretty well these days. I hope it lasts."

"That's great," said her new friend. "I look forward to having you join us."

"Thank you for having me. Unless I can help others, I feel lost." Samantha answered with a smile.

As they continued to discuss the morning's plan, Frank and Naomi walked into the shop and ordered their coffee drinks. After a few minutes, they joined Julius and Samantha at the table.

"Good morning," said Frank.

"Hi there," said Naomi. "It's good to see you again, Samantha. You're looking radiant."

Samantha hugged Naomi.

"How did you know I needed to hear that. Thank you," said Samantha.

Julius began to brief the team. Most of their meetings were held at this casual coffee spot.

"Well, as you know (motioning to Frank and Naomi), Samantha will join our team during her period of wellness. She's expressed a deep interest in being a part of what we do. She has a heart, even during her crisis and personal battle, to share happiness, joy, and comfort with patients at the medical center."

He picked up his cup of coffee and sipped it carefully before he continued.

"At Compassion United, we are pleased to have her on board for as long as she can. And I'll closely assess her physical state to be sure her health is not in jeopardy. Not in any way, shape, or form."

Julius spoke with tenderness and authority. He was a striking figure of poise and inner strength. He continued to speak after he focused his attention on Samantha.

"You're very important to me and I'll stand with you—we all will—during the rest of your days. And I hope that they are many. That they are lifetimes."

Samantha could not help herself but stare deeply into his eyes as he spoke those last several words. She was almost in a trance and taken back. Then she caught herself and chuckled.

"Uh, excuse me. Sorry. But you have a way with words," she said. "I'm very touched."

She smiled at her present company. Even if she had the strength to walk alongside these few for a short time, it would be well worth it.

Julius and the others left the shop armed with a day's worth of encouragement and of goodness to share with those fighting for their lives. They climbed in one car and were supplied with armfuls of donated blankets to personally hand out. Samantha was proud to be in their company and to be on their side of giving to others. She was a unique person who, on one hand, was fighting the very crisis she was about to comfort others stricken with, and on the other hand, desperately needed the comfort. Being with these gentle and loving teammates infused her with a new strength she did not expect to have. She always thought this course of her life in combat with Stillwhorm would look different for her. She imagined this time would be filled with despair and utter loneliness.

Samantha had a renewed sense of vision for her and Dominic. These days were brighter and held lofty expectations. But, she also knew the cold realities of this powerful agent of evil—Stillwhorm Syndrome. How it was ruthless and ravaged lives for years and years before. She was not a new victim to its wrath. And her level of respect for it had its secure place within her mind.

Unfortunately for her, that is precisely where Stillwhorm creates a foundation for victory over life. It begins in the mind. From there it slowly transforms any sense of good and hope into fragments of mere shattered dreams. This villain was not only out to destroy the fabric of life physically, but also to raise its might in the realm of mental capacity. If it can take the heart of someone early with cold cries of fear, then the rest of its decay would follow suit. For it is the physical that follows the imprisonment of the mind.

Hours later Samantha met Dominic at the heart of the school. His day was about to end and he was exhausted. Parents were allowed to meet their children in the large courtyard if they preferred. It felt more like a park setting than a school. The perimeter was outlined with trees and shrubs, and when the days were looked down upon by a smiling sun the courtyard was as bright as a glorious new day.

"Hello my sweet boy," said Samantha to Dominic as he hurried over to her holding a fistful of drawings and classwork he did that day. He jumped into her open arms as she kneeled.

"Hi, Mommy! Look what I did today."

He showed her his alphabet exercises with enthusiasm.

"Oh my," the proud mother said. "These are breathtaking!"

Dominic giggled at her remark. Even though he didn't know the meaning of what she had said, he believed her.

"Are we going home? I'm hungry," said a wide-eyed Dominic.

"No. I thought we'd go to eat pizza and some ice cream afterward," she said with a grin.

"Max's Pizza. Yay!"

He shouted with both hands raised in the air.

"I know they're your favorite," she said.

Samantha did not have to convince Dominic one ounce because he loved both places a great deal. He enjoyed it when his father would run up and down the aisle carrying him over his shoulders like he was an airplane just before Max himself would deliver his best pie to their table. Samantha would pretend to be the airport terminal calling them in for a landing just as the pizza was brought to the table. These were the moments Dominic wished he could have back. When he was with both of his parents laughing and being a happy family.

"Let's go," Dominic urged as he pulled her up from her kneeling position and guided her to their car.

She laughed and cherished his youthful charm. In the back of her mind, she told herself. *He's going to miss me dearly just like he misses Russell. Make every moment count.*

The pizza parlor was quiet because it was too early for the dinner crowds. This was perfect because Max, the owner, and master pie chef, was able to spend a few minutes with Samantha and Dominic. He rushed over to their table just as they sat in their booth.

"Well hello there, Sam and Dominic, my two favorite customers."

Max was cheery and upbeat. Behind his long white apron was a large man who consumed more of his creations than he should. His white t-shirt was pulled tightly over his wide belly and his voice was as deep as a well. His enormous dark mustache bounced and widened as he spoke, as it concealed his lips.

"What shall I get for you today?"

"I want pizza, Max!" Dominic couldn't hold it in any longer. "You know, a big cheese one and milk, please."

As the excited boy gave his order, he held up both arms in a round shape to help make his point. His cheery demeanor made Max's day.

"Oh, of course. Anything for you Dominic. What else, Sam?" he asked as he put two place settings down with neatly folded napkins and silverware.

"I'll have a house salad with ranch dressing. And water for me, please," she answered.

Max grinned right back at them.

"I'll make sure it's my best pie. How does that sound, Dominic?"

"Goodie," said Dominic, who already placed his napkin in his lap.

"I'll be right back with your drinks," said Max, then he turned and rushed to the kitchen.

He returned shortly after with a glass of water with ice and a cold glass of milk.

"Your food won't take long."

"Thanks," said Samantha.

Everything seemed to be in its place. Samantha felt well, she had a remarkable first day with Julius, Frank, and Naomi, and Dominic had a great first day of school. The only thing missing was her husband. She stared outside of the restaurant's window as if she was looking for Russell to suddenly appear out of thin air.

"Tell me about your first day, Dommie," she forced herself out of a downward emotional spiral and focused on her son. "I want to hear about everything."

Dominic adjusted himself in the booth and sat upright before he spoke.

"My teacher is Mrs. Hahn and she has a small mouth. But her voice is really loud when she talks."

Samantha laughed.

"We took turns saying our name and favorite animal," he said.

Amused, Samantha asked, "And what did you say?"

"I said Dominic Parsons and a crow," he answered.

She did not expect his answer and frowned slightly.

"I thought your name was Freddie Fun face and your favorite animal is a frog," she said in a silly tone.

"Mommy. Stop it," he giggled then took a drink of his milk.

"But really. Why a crow?" she asked.

"Well," he began to explain, "Because of the picnic with Dani. Those crows were nice to us."

She was puzzled at his newfound interest in crows. Especially at the eerie moment, they experienced while on that country picnic. She thought it was more traumatizing than nice, to say the least. She found those crows to be odd.

"Well, I hope you're not going to ask me if you can have one for a pet," she said jokingly.

"No," he said. "I don't need to."

She was a bit relieved but played it off well in front of him.

"I see. Maybe a goldfish would be better," she said.

"I already have one," he blurted.

"Have one what?" she asked.

"I already have a crow," he said in a matter-of-fact tone. "It's with me every day."

"Dommie, I don't understand," she said. "What do you mean?"

"A crow comes to my window. It sits there. Or, when I play outside it visits me," he said.

"Alright, that's strange," she said. "Why didn't you tell me this before? Why would a wild bird do that? Tell me when this happens again, okay?"

"Not if you're gonna make it go away," he answered.

"No. I'm just curious. That's all," she said.

After he thought about it for a moment he replied.

"Okay."

He had the childhood innocence that could easily make friends with make-believe characters or animals he considered friendly. And a crow was no different. Especially this one.

They continued to talk about his day and all the fun he had to make new friends. But it was the sound of someone mimicking an airplane that caught their attention. Max walked out of the kitchen holding a large round tin and on top of it was his cheese pizza masterpiece. He pretended it was a soaring plane ready to make its landing onto their table.

Dominic laughed at Max's goofiness. It reminded him of his father. And that was terrific.

"Thanks," said Dominic. "Good landing."

"I know you'll enjoy it, Dominic," replied the pizza chef. "If there's anything else I can bring you both please let me know."

Just as he finished his statement, another employee delivered Samantha's house salad.

"Thank you," said Samantha. "Everything looks tasty."

Dominic dove into his huge slice of Max's cheese creation. Since it was still hot, he took sips of his milk and fanned it with his napkin. It was a celebration meal on a special day. Samantha was happy. Not many days would look like this and she was well aware of that fact. So, each day was taken in with a thankful heart. Max's pizza was a cherry on top.

After their meal, they drove to Mr. Clark's ice cream shop. Dominic always had room for a scoop on a cake cone. They both sat there talking with Mr. Clark about his first day of school, the lovely weather, and his wife's fight with her terminal illness. She had not been doing well lately and spent more days and nights at the medical center. His countenance became sad as he spoke about his wife's troubles. His heart was in severe pain because he had to endure watching her life fade away.

"I hate Stillwhorm," he said with anger and swollen eyes. "I hate everything about this dreadful sickness. Just when I thought she'd turned a corner for the better, she got worse."

He didn't mean to scare Dominic with his raw emotions and he smiled suddenly at them both as he wiped his eyes.

"I'm sorry. I don't mean to trouble you with our issues."

"No, it's alright," said Samantha compassionately. "I completely understand, I do."

She let out a smile and gave him a long hug.

"We're here for you. I can prepare some meals for you both and bring them by tomorrow. How does that sound?"

He appreciated her gesture and her warmth. They made him feel better.

"Well, thank you. I'd love that," he said.

"So, we'll be by your place tomorrow around five, alright? You send her our love."

"Goodbye," said Dominic while he hugged the broken man. Dominic always considered Mr. Clark as a type of grandfather figure.

"Thank you. You take good care of your mother, now," said Mr. Clark as he patted Dominic on the head.

They both left with a new heaviness on their hearts. At every turn in their lives, there was someone stricken with this dreadful disease.

Later that evening, Dani came over to see how Dominic's first day of school went. She brought him a new box of vibrant markers and a coloring book with animals and sea creatures. They all huddled around the dinner table and laughed. Dani always brought the best out of Samantha and she did her best to uplift her friend with every visit.

Samantha shared with her friend those details concerning Mrs. Clark's health problems. More reminders of what was sure to come for her. And with Samantha's life on the other side of her wish transfer, her reality was now established within the confines of time. Her days were numbered and with fewer days than if she had not traded her life for her son. The complexity of living under the duress of that looming death sentence was torture.

But she also felt a lift that was priceless from her new alliance with Compassion United. Samantha quickly turned the conversation from dread to hope by telling Dani how wonderful her first day was with Julius, Frank, and Naomi.

"I felt so alive today," said Samantha. "It's difficult to explain. It was so fulfilling."

"That's wonderful," said Dani. "I appreciate them."

"Yeah. Me too," Samantha agreed then she glanced over to the neighboring room to be sure Dominic wasn't there. "Dani, I'm not sure how much time I have," she said in a whisper, "but if I can continue to be healthy enough for this act of service I'll be in a better place emotionally. This is going to help me get through this."

Dani grabbed her friend's hand and looked her directly in her eyes.

"You're an amazing person and the best friend anyone could ever have. You inspire me," said Dani.

They spent the duration of the evening sharing laughs and a few tears. Meanwhile, Dominic was occupied in his room. He explored his new coloring book and with every page, he infused life with his markers. Images of pale black and white outlines became realistic animals that jumped from the page. He could spend much of his time alone and be completely satisfied.

While he sat at his walnut desk beneath his desktop lamp that illuminated his work area with warm light, he was lost in a world of imagination. While he continued to color the animal images, his mind danced with make-believe. Then, he turned the page after completing the last image and his eyes focused intently on what he saw. It was a crow on the page perched on a tree limb. He believed it was an outline of the very crow that visits him. He was amused.

He looked at the carton of markers to select the colors necessary for this special page. He grabbed midnight black, forest brown, and slate grey to begin his quest. As he began to apply rich colors to the paper, he felt more and more comfortable as he sat there. His feet began to tap each other as if his favorite song was playing. He swayed his head from left to right and repeated; he was in a groove and completely enthralled at the moment.

He spoke to the image on paper.

"Hi, crow. I'm making you fly and live with these colors. Like the real crow that visits me."

He mixed deep black, brown, and grey in strokes that mimicked the feathers and wings. He carefully stayed within the lines and he took more time with this image in contrast to the other animals he colored. After the crow was filled with the dark hues, he picked some more markers and started filling in the tree limb. His ability as a young artist was advanced.

"You are the tree the crows protect," he said with an unmistakable confidence. "You're strong and you have special fruit. It gives life. And your name is Mara."

After a slight pause, he selected a whole variety of colors. Then, one at a time, he began to apply color to the tree and its limbs. It wasn't only tans and browns like most tree trunks. This one was different and unique; Dominic had a sense of realism about Mara without ever seeing it. Then he smiled because he was pleased with his accomplishment.

No one had ever shared the details of Mara and its mysterious life-giving source with Dominic. Nor the crows that were dedicated in service to this mighty tree of life. But, how did he suddenly know these particular details? And why was he visited regularly by the crow he considered his friend? These realities were now revealed to him since his mother's wish transfer; he had sipped from the sacred nectar and since that moment he began to receive revelation. Perhaps placed intentionally in his mind for his future, for his purpose. Until those days ahead occurred, he continued playing the role of a little boy who loved his mother and wanted nothing else but to enjoy the simplistic moments in life. He knew the gravity of his mother's gift and with that, he would not take a second of breath for granted.

Later that night, Dominic slept comfortably in his bed. He kept the night light on that his mother placed near his bedside and he made sure his drapes were open. He wanted his crow to have visible access into the bedroom.

Hours into the boy's sleep, he began to have a vivid dream. One that seemed so very real. As the scene unfolded, he realized that it took place in his room. The details began to emerge.

It was nighttime and Dominic was asleep. The crow faithfully kept watching through his window as it stood outside on the sill. It was quiet and on guard. Until something caught the crow's attention. Something was moving inside of the room.

Slowly, the edge of Dominic's bedroom door crept open as if someone pushed it from the other side. There were many times during the night when Samantha couldn't sleep and she would walk to his room and check on him. The crow's vision was acute in the darkness, even from its position outside. It focused directly on the door's movement and waited for a likeness of his mother to appear.

Then, a tall figure appeared in the darkness moving slowly from behind the door and into the room. It was Clyde and his stench now confirmed the crow's suspicion. He stood there staring and paused in a moment of certain victory from the position of attack he had now gained over Samantha's child. The blackness in his eyes revealed the frantic gaze of a madman. Even the softly lit dimness of the night light illuminated his face. The crow began to caw and take several flaps with its wings as it hovered in a frenzy.

Clyde then surged forward as a lion leaps forward to pounce on its prey. He glided through the air as he took giant steps and quickly glided towards Dominic who remained asleep.

Suddenly, something pierced through the window from outside with blazing speed. The crash through the windowpane startled Dominic and within a flash, Clyde was immediately thrust against the wall beside the bed. The crow had broken through the glass like a bullet and crashed into the attacker with raging force, deflecting Clyde's momentum towards the boy. Dominic screamed as he saw the intruder pinned against the wall being viciously attacked by the crow.

Clyde was outmatched by the crow's fury and flailed his arms to mount a defense. But the crow overcame the attacker and began to slash every part of his flesh to shreds with unrelenting punishment. The crow unleashed its power to protect the boy. In a matter of seconds, it was over.

Dominic breathed hysterically then he opened his eyes as he sat up against his headboard holding his blanket up to his chest. He began to cry from the traumatic dream.

He looked around his room anxiously. His chest was heaving up and down as if he was running full speed. *It was a dream* he told himself. Clyde was not there. He looked over to both sides of his bed to see if anyone was on the floor. But there was no one. He jumped out of his bed and hurried to his window. The crow was outside alert and ready. He was barely visible from the low light of the moon that evening, but surely he was there guarding Dominic. They looked at each other and the boy put his hand on the glass and smiled. It was a gesture of gratitude. The crow pecked the other side of the glass to show him it understood.

Dominic stood by the window for a better part of the hour. The seemingly real attack from Clyde rattled him. It was difficult to go back to sleep right away. Instead, he stared curiously at his guardian crow. And Dominic knew he was safe.

CHAPTER 9

Under grayish blue skies, many family members and friends gathered to honor Mrs. Clark. The sprawling grass was deep green and clusters of granite tombstone markers occupied the hillside. A slight breeze passed over the gathering as if it brought waves of comfort. Small rows of black metal chairs were positioned before a closed casket and a bountiful display of flowers. James Clark held his wife's picture in his hands and a red rose as he sat with the other members of their family in the front row. She was the love of his life and separated by her passing left him nauseated with grief.

Samantha was there too. She stood behind the gathering along with Dani. Dominic was with a sitter. She remembered how sweet Mrs. Clark was towards her and Dominic. Her lovely memories of this loving woman were in abundance because she enjoyed making people feel terrific. It was her legacy and everyone who knew her remembered their friend as a woman of strength and poise. Through her last several months of illness, Mrs. Clark held onto the goodness of her life and demonstrated kindness just as she did during those years of her health. Her circumstance did not cloud her joy of living or prevent her smile from lighting other's faces. Samantha learned a great deal from Mrs. Clark and in observing her suffering, she hoped she could live her final days in just the same manner. Because Samantha knew her end was coming.

The sobbing echoed across the assembly of loved ones. Their cries reminded Samantha of her husband's service and how at such a young age he was taken from his family. Mrs. Clark lived to be seventy-two before she breathed her last. And that was quite a long time to live; the unforgiving disease did not strike her in her earlier years. A gracious man, Mr. Clark, appreciated every moment with his bride. He didn't let his favorite picture out of his grasp throughout the entire day.

At the end of the service, the groups of loved ones began to unravel. The quiet words of consolation and hugs were shared. The group began their departure and headed to the Clark residence, including Dani and Samantha.

"Do you mind walking ahead of me to the car and wait for me?" Samantha said with somberness. "I just need a few moments alone."

"No problem," replied Dani. "Take as long as you need."

She turned and walked towards their parked car.

Samantha guided herself through the stretch of green grass and tombstones until she found Russell's gravesite. But she stopped short of it in fear that she would become too overwhelmed with grief. From a distance, her eyes were fixed at his granite stone that marked his physical resting place. She folded her arms tightly as a chill was felt throughout her body. The broken widow became very uncomfortable and suddenly unsettled. Just then, a stale voice called from behind her.

"Samantha."

Clyde had been present the entire time and stood in the background away from her view. He carefully approached her as if he were stalking his prey.

"Why have you attended this solemn service? I'm surprised to see you here under these dark circumstances," he said.

He nodded to Samantha as she turned to face him.

"I have nothing to say to you," she said.

"Oh, but you should. I am the only one who truly understands your pain. I freely give it and I freely take it away."

His voice caused her fear to rise. That was his plan.

"Leave me alone," she demanded.

She quickly made her escape away from him. Clyde remained motionless after her sudden departure. He stared towards space she just occupied for a few moments, then he turned his eyes at her retreating figure. His stare burned into the afternoon's gloom before he left the cemetery himself. Along the way, he read many of the tombstones and the names of those who had departed. Many of whom he recognized. Many of them he distinctly remembered their pain and their suffering. After all, it was his personal touch that infected each one of their lives. At least those who died from Stillwhorm Syndrome.

"That man is back," Samantha blurted to her friend after getting into Dani's car.

"What man?" Dani asked with concern as she scanned the cemetery. "I don't see anyone."

"He's right there by that cluster of trees staring at us," said Samantha.

Her breathing became erratic and panicked. Samantha pointed to where Clyde was as she tapped the car window emphatically. He stood there about fifty yards away with a cold glare and eyes of bitterness towards Samantha.

"You don't see him? He's right there! That jerk who came to my house," Samantha said with frustration.

"Hey, I'll get help," said Dani. "I'll drive us to the main office. But, honestly Sam, I don't see him."

"No. It's alright." Samantha eased into her seat and turned on the radio. "Let's just get out of here."

They drove through the winding road that lined the memorial garden. She began to calm down and she reassured herself. Occasionally, her head turned back to see if he followed until they left the grounds.

What Samantha did not realize is that Clyde could only reveal himself to those whom he chose. He was a physical manifestation of Stillwhorm Syndrome itself. But contained in a human form with tissue and matter; a walking and talking foreign being among other people. If he stood in a crowded room where Samantha was, she would be the only person with eyes to see him. He usually slid through the land concealed by the wind and the air invisible to everyone. Everyone except for Mara and the crows, who were able to see him with ease.

His power consisted of these attributes. He was not invincible, yet he had abilities no human could possess. Clyde rose from a source of evil that opposed all that was good and pure in the land. He was a nemesis to Mara; an adversary to perfect goodness. But good was far more dominant.

Now it was his time to punish Samantha. He waited from behind the scenes throughout her lifetime for a specific moment when he could attack. But the presence of her protection provided through her Petitioners continued to guard her life. Until the moment she drank from the sacred and bonded with the wish transfer willingly, then she opened herself to his vicious poison. The window of opportunity was his for the taking.

Clyde would manifest himself in his human form during this time of her punishment. The times when she could look into his eyes made his pursuit of victory even sweeter, like a predator that witnesses its victim's life escaping through its expression. He eagerly desired to observe Samantha stricken with horror at the sight of her demise. And he savored every moment.

But, this was not the fullness of his capability. No, he had other ways he could inflict her; other methods to pummel with his vengeance. Until she breathed her last ounce of air. And he would not stop until she was lifeless.

~

Weeks had compiled terrific days for Samantha and Dominic. The school was a bright part of his weekly schedule and he thoroughly enjoyed learning, participating, and playing with friends in his classroom. For Samantha, having several hours a day while he attended class meant she could spend much of that time serving with the Compassion United team and she did so for these past weeks.

Julius poured into her during their volunteer service at the medical center, but she didn't fully realize this. In her mind, she gave to those who suffered in treatment and with that dedication to them, her life was made full. With every contact, Julius made specific comments concerning the afflicted ones they visited. Comments of encouragement, peace, and gracious love to brighten the dark corners where they each fought for their lives. And with his delivery of such elevating words, he purposed them to also fall upon Samantha's ears since she was at his side. Sure, he focused upon each patient during these moments, but he meant for every gesture and word to pour over into her life as well. It was a collateral blessing. Little did she know that his effect on her inner person forged new strength and raised her to heights she had not experienced.

It was exactly what she needed. And all the while Julius had insight into her needs. Perhaps it was due to his years of experience with these patients. Even though he wasn't a man of middle age or he didn't earn decades of experience in this field, his short time being a minister of hope to the critically ill created vast layers of knowledge and depths of compassion. He was a savior to her. Saving her from the dark bitterness that befalls those who contract Stillwhorm.

Typically, from the onset of this calamity, many fall into a deep depression difficult to climb out of. But, Samantha had not experienced that level of depression. Sure, she found herself fighting against the grief from losing her husband and the truth concerning her end, but most of these weeks she was upbeat and gained hope for each new day.

But on this day, the second day of her fifth-week post-onset of the Stillwhorm attack, she hit a wall physically. She opened her eyes in the morning and knew exactly what the feeling in her bones meant. It was going to be a hard and trying day with her sickness, to say the least. She assessed her day ahead and strategically thought about how best to navigate Dominic's school schedule. Samantha had to get over to the clinic early and see Dr. Brimmer.

She picked up her phone and called Dani.

"Hey."

"What's wrong?" Dani replied.

"Can you take Dommie to school for me? I know it's last minute and you've got work too. I don't feel well," said Samantha.

"Listen. You make sure he's ready and I'll pick him up. No problem at all. But are you okay?" Dani said with concern. "How bad do you feel?"

"I'll be alright," Samantha replied. "I just know what kind of day I'm going to have. You know, one that will likely be spent on a hospital bed. But I feel fine enough to get him ready. Thank you."

"See you in about twenty-five minutes," said Dani.

And with the beginning of a new day that was shaped to become one steeped with suffering, Samantha arrived at the medical center for a clinic appointment she had quickly scheduled. She thanked the front desk team for allowing her to arrive at such short notice and walked back to an exam room after the nurse called her name. She sat and waited briefly for Dr. Brimmer in the quiet patient room.

"Well, hello Sam," Dr. Brimmer said cheerfully as he opened the door and entered the room. "What brings you in so urgently today?"

"I know it," she said then hesitated. "I just know it. I feel it in my body."

"Okay. Tell me what you're feeling this morning so we can take care of you," he replied.

She held her hand cupped to her forehead and misery was plastered all over her face.

"My bones are hurting. Like pain from deep within my tissues, I've not felt before. And I find myself having shortness of breath occasionally."

The doctor looked concerned but tried to hide it from her.

"May I examine your neck area?" he asked.

"Sure," Samantha said with fatigue setting in.

He began to run his fingers delicately along the sides of her neck, feeling for any signs of exaggerated lymph node swelling very common with Stillwhorm. He looked beyond her head to the wall behind her as he focused on his sense of touch. His hands moved upwards closer to her jawline then he closed his eyes for a moment as he put his hands down at his side.

"We must get you to a treatment room," he opened his eyes and looked at her with seriousness.

"What is it?" she asked.

He turned to open the door and called for a nurse.

"Jan. Can you get a room ready for Samantha now?"

He looked back at her and opened his chart.

"Your condition appears to be in its second stage now, I'm afraid. We're getting you to a room where we'll start a much stronger medication. Is anyone able to care for Dominic? Maybe your friend?"

Nurse Jan walked in and notified the doctor they were ready for her. Everything was moving so fast for her troubled mind.

"Uh, yeah. Dani will pick him up from school later and watch him," said Samantha with a frown. "What does this mean?"

He took down some notes in her chart and didn't respond. She asked again.

"Doctor, what does this mean?"

He stopped writing and turned his attention to her.

"You're advancing rapidly to the next phase of Stillwhorm. Just before the end stage appears. Soon the sickness will attack with increased fury. I'm sorry."

She knew this day would arrive. The day to end all days was near. And his words echoed between her ears. She tried to shut out his voice from her mind to no avail. This news struck her like the brutal force windstorm of a hurricane. She suddenly felt lonely, defenseless, and afraid.

Jan returned to escort Samantha back to the treatment wing.

"Let's take you back," said Jan.

She paused for a few seconds, then acknowledged the nurse.

"Um. Yeah."

Dr. Brimmer gave Jan the medication and rate of infusion.

"Let's start her on the first cycle immediately and check vitals every fifteen minutes, please," he said. "I really would like to see how she's doing with this at the end of two hours. If I need to adjust anything I can do so early."

He turned to Samantha and reassured her.

"We're going to do everything we can. Okay?"

She agreed and followed the nurse to her room. As they walked through the long hallway, they passed several rooms, some of which had their doors ajar. Samantha fell behind as she glanced into some of the rooms. She recognized patient's faces from her recent volunteer time with the CU team. It was an awkward feeling.

"And here you go, Samantha," the nurse offered her a private room. "I'll be right back with everything we need to begin."

The nurse hurried out of the room.

In that silent minute, everything seemed clear. As if voices were speaking to her within ten feet from her bed. They pulled her into the belief that she was entering the final stretch of her battle with this illness. There was no turning back now. She rubbed her arms because of the throbbing pain from deep within. The assault on her body was in perfect concert with the attack on her mind.

The infusion began shortly after she settled in. And just like clockwork, Nurse Jan checked in on her and recorded her vitals.

"You're doing well," said the nurse. This round of medication may make you feel tired and sleepy. So, if you need to rest and close your eyes go right ahead."

"Thank you. I just might do that," said Samantha.

The mechanical pump was the only audible source in her room. The rhythmic heartbeat of the machine proved to be calming somehow. She focused on the internal churning of switches and gears that pushed the IV medication into her body. Was this pump an ally or an enemy? The medicine began to nauseate Samantha. She squirmed in her bed and pulled the paper-thin blanket over her shoulder as she slumped into a slumber. It felt like poison introduced into her bloodstream. She closed her eyes and thought about her son's life. It was a happy thought that coated her discomfort.

In her mind, she could hear his laughter as if Dominic was right by her side. In a dream-like state, she wandered away from distress and looked into his eyes. Her child's eyes only expressed love. His tranquil expression eased her pain. She began to dance with him in their private garden. They twirled beneath the sunshine's rays and simply delighted in each other. It was bliss.

And suddenly, just as an earthquake rocks the ground without warning, something violently broke through her peaceful moment. A voice she could not put out of her head had come as an uninvited guest. It was Clyde.

The sinister one entered her moment of serenity as effortlessly as a dolphin glides through tamed oceans. Clyde stepped into her dream state with his unique power—another ability in his arsenal. He could whisper lies and deceit within this realm, in a way to offer deceptive persuasion. As well as physically make contact with her to some degree—only if she was willing.

"Samantha."

His coldness was conveyed even in his spoken word.

"Why do you continue to resist the inevitable? Your path leads to your demise. You chose this."

She felt a chill run through her body as he spoke among the silence. With each of his words, the chill pulsated with intensity, in synchronicity with Clyde's verbal cadence. It felt almost as if he somehow was invading her vascular system. Her eyes remained closed in her state of in-between.

"Will you allow me to end your pain once and for all? This game you're playing is pitiful. Stop fighting me."

Clyde continued to convince Samantha with his tickling words.

"Let go and let me bring you into the afterlife. Don't you miss Russell? You can be with him this very minute. Take my hand and I will show you how."

She processed his offer. It was enticing. She would enjoy removing herself from this calamity knowing that her battle would only increase in agonizing pain. *Why continue in this suffering?* She asked herself. *I don't want Dominic to see me crumble and pass away in misery just like he did with his father. Maybe this will be the better way to leave him. A short and abrupt departure.* She wrestled with Clyde's suggestion. She began to let go of her fight within and take his hand to end this madness.

"There, there, my dear. I will bring an end to your suffering."

Clyde's devious grin was undeniable. He was proud of his evil enticement. He thoroughly enjoyed his purpose.

Samantha was fully incapacitated by now. She laid there helplessly in a trance of his persuasion. But a new presence overwhelmed this dark moment. A new figure entered the room. And he brought with him the brilliance of life itself.

"Samantha?"

Julius softly called to her as he tapped on her wall. Instantly, she responded to the sound of his voice. It was calming. Just as a gentle movement of flowing waters.

Her eyes opened and she turned her head to see his face, but she couldn't speak. It felt like paralysis overtook her speech. She smiled back at Julius.

"The door was slightly ajar, so I walked in. I wanted to see you," he said.

He walked over to her side and sat down. He brought a new quilt that he began to drape over her body. The comfort he brought felt like the warmest sunshine on a cold, blustery day. Immediately, Clyde's voice and presence disappeared. Julius's radiance was more powerful by far.

"I heard you were admitted this morning," he continued to softly speak. "I'm sorry for this road you must endure. Keep your eyes on today, Samantha, just today. Together we will get through today."

Her heart was delivered from turmoil and her physical pain, although was there, seemed almost as a distant pestering instead. She felt guarded by his presence and encouraged by his essence. He sat with her for hours into the late morning.

The infusion was recalculated by Dr. Brimmer and, unfortunately, it was determined that her progression was far worse than he anticipated. She would have to remain hospitalized for at least a few days. The treatment would make her weak and frail, but it was necessary for the attempt to perhaps stave off the inevitable.

Julius remained constantly with her well into the afternoon and she perked up some. And, after she was able to eat a small meal and drink some tea, she had new guests arrive. Dani picked up Dominic from school and they walked in to bring another layer of happiness to Samantha's day.

"Hey you two," Samantha said, still feeling weakened.

They both came alongside her and Dominic gave her a sweet hug. His tenderness was unequaled and her devotion was unrivaled.

The room was filled with perfect love. Everyone surrounded Samantha in her toughest day so far. It was as good as it could get for her considering all the circumstances. Although she would much rather be in the comfort of her home, at least she had the sweet company of Dominic, Dani, and Julius. And that was as perfect as it could be.

Thirty-three Crows

CHAPTER 10

August 18, Wednesday

D r. Brimmer had been closely analyzing Samantha's blood test results for three days while she remained hospitalized. In-patient status was necessary to monitor her and support her medical frailty. The findings were less than desirable. They were alarming. Stillwhorm Syndrome was on a rampage through her system and the disease was about to wreak havoc on her organs.

He was deeply saddened by this latest round of results. He had witnessed countless victims fall to this sickness in his career as a physician. But when it strikes the people he knows and admires it becomes very personal. Samantha was not his sole patient, but a friend whom he admired greatly. It wrecked his heart that he couldn't rescue her from the clutches of this wicked enemy. For some reason, it was consuming her more rapidly than originally diagnosed upon her admission. All he could do was his best to keep her alive as long as he could.

He wrote new orders for the medication used during the last phase of the disease. It was Miquelten. The purpose was to strengthen her remaining white blood cells, arm them with one final defense, to give her a little more time with her loved ones.

This medication was not a means to cure her because that was impossible, but to buy her a few more days at best. He had to break the news to her that day.

~

Dominic walked into the kitchen fully dressed and with a full appetite. Dani already was preparing breakfast for them both. She had temporarily moved in at Samantha's house to care for Dominic.

"Hey champ," she greeted him still holding the spatula. "You hungry for my world-famous, chocolate chip pancakes?"

"Okay," he answered.

Dominic was sad for his mother. He missed having her at home every day. These last few days brought back fresh memories from a year ago when his father was fighting the same illness. He couldn't help but think about living without either of his parents. It was a heavy load to bear for a child.

Dani paused and stepped closer to him. She crouched down to look him in the eye as she reassured him.

"I know this is so hard for you. But I'm right here. I'll take care of you."

She held him and he felt safe.

"I want her to get better," Dominic said in a whisper but very audible to her.

She kissed him on the top of his thick head of hair and resumed her position at the stove.

"We're going to eat until we're stuffed and then head over to see your mom," she said. "It's going to be a good day. You'll see."

He kept his favorite animal from the coloring book in his lap. He carefully cut a single page of the crow from the book and carried it around with him. During breakfast, he rested it on his lap while he ate. Some children prefer to tote stuffed animals,

123

little plastic figures, or small toys. Dominic favored his colored sheet of paper of a crow. He knew it was his friend and guardian.

After their meal together, they cleaned up and prepared for another visit with Samantha. Dominic held a small brown paper bag as he walked out of the house and into the backyard. He was on a mission that required him to venture into his mother's favorite place—her peaceful garden. His eyes scanned every flower and every shrub for a bouquet he could collect for his mother. He knew it would brighten her day and that was all he wanted to accomplish. Just to brighten her day.

After a brief walk, he found some colorful flowers he decided to cut. He pulled a small pair of scissors from his jacket pocket and carefully cut the stems about nine inches down from the blossom. Dani stood quietly in the background watching. He placed them into the bag and continued his walk through the garden. When he found some daisies he clipped them as well to add to his collection. The flowers were a perfect gift for his mother.

He wrapped the middle of the bag with a pink ribbon he found in his mother's room and tied a knot with a bow. Dominic used the same method as when he tied his shoelaces. When he was satisfied he turned and started back to the house, when something caught his attention. It was his crow, the one that watched over him. He stopped and looked over his shoulder to where it was perched. Dominic waved at it and smiled. The crow responded with a loud caw and a flutter of his wings. After a few seconds of admiring the bird, Dominic resumed his walk to the house. It was time to leave and see his mother.

Dani looked at his exchange with the crow with great curiosity. She thought it was strange that a wild bird would continue to come around the house. Specifically, to come around where Dominic was.

"You ready?" she asked as she held the door open for him.

"Yup."

Proud of his gift, he answered with certainty.

"Oh, she's going to love those," said Dani.

They buckled up and started for the medical center. The car sped down the main road towards town and Dani played upbeat music. She loved to sing while she drove and sometimes Dominic joined in. She made the drive as positive as she could. And all the while as they passed through the rural area, the crow was following from the skies above. It flew in pursuit but not as a predator—as an impressive protector.

"Good morning, sunshine," Samantha's nurse greeted her as she walked into her room. The shift changed just occurred and the day shift team was preparing their patients for the day.

Samantha was already awake and had her lights and the television on.

"Hmmm," she cleared her throat before saying her first words that day.

"Morning, Robin."

"You look like you've already started your morning."

Nurse Robin always kept a brilliant smile as she spoke to Samantha.

"I have your new meds ready for your infusion. Would you like to wait until after you eat to begin?"

"New meds?" Samantha asked. "What new medication am I taking?"

"Well, I thought you were told, but you weren't. Let me get Dr. Brimmer," she said.

Robin continued to take her vitals and record them in her chart.

"Alright. Yeah, I'll eat first before the meds."

Samantha's voice was tired still. The last three days had taken their toll on her physically.

"How about oatmeal and tea, please?"

"Of course. I'll get that ordered right away."

The nurse moved with purpose and left the room.

Samantha remained in her bed with her head resting on the pillow. The television was on but she didn't pay any attention to the movie that played. The sound was hardly enough to combat her feelings of being alone. But it was all she had when there were no visitors. She looked forward to seeing Dominic and Dani. Dani had taken two weeks of emergency vacation to care for Dominic and spend more time with Samantha. The weary patient was eternally grateful for her dear friend.

"Knock, knock," Dani said quietly as she peeked into her room.

"Hi, Mommy." Dominic said while he rushed over to her. "Look what I have for you?"

He proudly offered her his paper bag-wrapped bouquet.

"Good morning. Oh my, these are lovely."

Her expression changed from gloomy to sunny with their entrance. She pulled the freshly cut flowers close to her nose and enjoyed their sweet aroma. It was a delight compared with the staleness of the hospital air.

"Thank you, sweetie. I love them so much. And I love you."

Her smile was the proof of her heart's elation right at that moment. If she could capture that feeling and somehow summon it when she needed to, she would do so.

Dani walked over to her window and drew open the curtains. The morning light suddenly filled the room and delivered a new day's worth of hope. She walked over to the bed and brushed her friend's bangs away from her eyes. Dani was tender towards

Samantha. And it disturbed her greatly to witness her best friend being brutalized by such illness. She did everything she could to conceal her pain.

They both smiled deeply at each other.

"Thank you for being here," Samantha said.

"Nowhere else, my friend. You know," Dani replied.

"Mommy," Dominic's voice cut through the tender moment they shared. "I brought my coloring book and markers for later."

She turned towards him as he sat comfortably in the chair near the nightstand.

"That's great. You can change the channel and put on something you like."

After half an hour or so, Dr. Brimmer walked in to say hello to Samantha.

"Good morning Samantha. Hi there Dominic, Dani."

"Good morning," Samantha said.

"Hi," said Dominic and Dani.

"How are you feeling this morning?" asked the doctor. "Strong enough to get up out of bed today and sit in a chair?"

He urged with his best persuasion.

"I think so. Hey, what about this new medication I'm starting today?" she asked.

He hesitated and then asked Samantha with all seriousness.

"Yeah. Can I have a moment with you alone?"

"Sure," she answered. "Dani?" Samantha turned to her friend and without hesitation, she understood what Samantha meant.

"Hey, Dommie. Can we take a walk for a few minutes?" Dani extended her open hand out to him as she asked.

He jumped out of the chair and walked over to take her hand. Dani led him out of the room and Dr. Brimmer gently closed the door.

"Okay. Now you're scaring me, doctor," said Samantha.

Samantha tried to sit up to have what appeared to be a serious conversation coming. He pulled up a chair from across the room and sat right next to her.

"Samantha, the new drug we're starting today is meant for those patients in the last phase of their fight with Stillwhorm."

His words were sprinkled with as much mercy he could apply. These were words that all patients dreaded to hear. And delivering them was one of the toughest things he faced as a physician.

Samantha had a glazed look in her sullen eyes. As she comprehended the news he saw her tears begin to form. They welled up from deep within and the pale skin on her tired face began to tremble. She frowned and pounded her fist into the thin mattress.

"No. No."

She let out her anger. Her frustration had hit its peak. The timing of her cycle with Stillwhorm had become shorter than originally expected. She held her face with both hands as if to shield her sorrow from the world around her. She poured her pain directly into them.

Dr. Brimmer reached his hand to her and rested it on her shoulder.

"I'm terribly sorry. Please understand I'm doing everything humanly possible here. Everything we can to help you. But if we don't commence with this today, you might not make it through the next handful of hours."

She uncovered her face and remained quiet as she continued to absorb the information. He continued to explain the situation.

"I've closely studied the patterns in your blood work related to a specific type of protein and it reveals a looming attack on your organs very, very soon. But if we can begin the new infusion today, this morning, it can improve your immune system right now. The catch is this will probably only buy us a few more days of your best health. To spend with Dominic and Dani, with your friends and loved ones. We use this for a sudden boost in the body, but at the cost of an immediate collapse of the heart function shortly after it wears off. It does come at a cost."

She listened intently as he added more to his game plan.

"If you agree, we have this ready to go and I'll have Robin come in. I would like to offer you a few more good days instead of your final twenty-four hours of suffering. Listen, Samantha, if we don't do this now today will be your worst day and you won't make it through tomorrow. Again, I am very sorry to have to deliver this to you."

Dr. Brimmer was more serious than she had ever seen. But she also remembered Russell's end cycle of his fight. They chose the same medication and it did help provide him with two-and-a-half good days before he passed. Still, having a definitive timeframe of taking your last breath was extremely difficult to comprehend.

"I understand."

Her reply was mixed with tears, pain, and appreciation for all that he had done for her family. Finality has come and its poison stung with bitterness.

"Thank you, doctor, for everything. Let's do it."

He was put at ease by her warm character. There were few patients as tender and gracious as Samantha. She was truly one of a kind.

"Okay," he said quietly to her. "That's what we'll do."

Dr. Brimmer smiled and noticed the flowers in her lap.

"Those are beautiful. I'll place them in water for you."

She wiped her tears with new tissues and handed him her bouquet as she nodded. He took them and left her room. Robin didn't hesitate with the doctor's orders and she immediately brought a new bag of fluids and a bag of the new medication. The bags were hung on the IV pole and she began to prime the tubing before loading it into the pump.

"Hey kiddo," Robin said with an encouraging tone. "You're going to receive this over the next three hours and by about the halfway point you'll notice a big difference in your strength. Once I'm done here I'll bring in your breakfast and let you eat before we get started."

"Thank you, Robin," Samantha said. "You and the others here on this floor have been tremendous to me."

"Oh, sweetie. You're gonna make me cry," said Robin as she fanned her eyes quickly with both hands. "You're so welcome."

Once the tubing was ready, she hung the line up on the pole ready for the infusion. Robin made her quick exit then returned moments later with Samantha's food just as she had ordered. She placed the tray on the rolling table with an adjustable tray and slid it over her lap. It made for a perfect way to eat while in bed. Samantha used her hand-held remote to bring the bed in an upright position. She sipped her tea and mixed her berries into the oatmeal.

"Call me when you're done," said Robin before she walked out.

Every meal and every single cup of tea was a precious reminder of how much she loved her life. The peculiar details like a simple cup of hot tea became a tremendous memory she suddenly cherished. And since her days were numbered, each one of these moments over the next three days would become some of her new favorites.

"Hey Sam," Dani said as she held Dominic's hand and returned. "You okay?"

She continued to chew and swallow her spoonful of oatmeal she just put in her mouth. Then answered Dani.

"Listen. If you can sign up Dommie at the daycare center in the lobby later, we can talk. Maybe for just an hour or so." Samantha sipped her tea and smiled at Dani.

Samantha turned to Dominic.

"Did you have a nice walk?"

"Yup," he answered quickly. "But I want to sit in your bed now."

She pushed the tray out of the way and pulled back the covers on one side and he kicked off his shoes before climbing in bed with Samantha. He was as happy as could be right there in the comfort of her presence, her warmth. He pulled the covers up to his chin and smiled up towards her. And this mother cherished the perfection of the moment. She looked down on him with a longing to freeze time and have him at her side for as long as forever really is.

The morning hours sped as a wild horse gallops over open fields. Dani returned from taking Dominic to the daycare center and closed the door behind her.

"Okay, Sam. What is it?" Dani asked. "What did they tell you?"

Samantha cleared her throat and sat up a little more before she answered.

"Dr. Brimmer has been watching my labs closely over the last few days."

She paused and rubbed her forehead.

"I...I don't have much time now, Dani. The illness is now in its last stage. He told me I only had about a day before it attacks my organs."

Samantha trembled as she delivered the news.

Dani rushed over to her bed and held her best friend. Their sobbing was the only outcome of their brief conversation. The cries grew louder as they rocked side to side in their tight embrace. Dani couldn't bear the thought of losing Samantha so very soon.

Samantha spoke with her head resting on Dani's shoulder.

"They began infusing a medication to boost my immune system enough to buy me a few more good days. Then it's over."

"Well, we'll make these next few days the best possible," Dani said.

They settled into their embrace for quite a long time. The only sound for long periods was the running of the machine that infused strength into her body. After a while, they wiped their faces and discussed fun things to do.

"Hey, I need you," said Samantha but paused for a few moments. "I need you to take custody of Dommie for me."

Dani expected those words to be cast upon her heart. There was no one else Samantha could trust like her dearest friend.

"Of course, Sam. You know I'll do my very best for Dommie," Dani said.

They both sealed the deal with a hug and a precious smile. The remaining time was spent laughing about the hilarious memories they created. And after several hours of the new infusion, Samantha began to feel renewed. The pain in her tissues eased and became more of a slight ache. Her eyes didn't feel as heavy as they did. She had the urge to stand to her feet and walk into the hallway. The medicine was working.

~

The knocking reverberated throughout the chamber office. It disrupted the mood of silence and serenity. Not many visitors came to this place, which made Mr. Harshom extremely interested in who could be at the door. He slid his chair away from the desk and approached the main entry. He unlocked and opened the heavy security door.

An unusual pounding wind was relentless to the surrounding facility grounds. A hooded man stood there on the other side impaled by the winds. Mr. Harshom stared for a moment then he recognized the person.

"What brings you here?" Mr. Harshom asked.

"I need to talk to you," said the man speaking loudly over the screaming, gusty winds. "It's urgent."

"Of course. Come in."

He stepped aside to let his guest in, then closed and locked the door. They walked over to a table and began their lengthy conversation.

The outside calamity unleashed its continued fury. And inside, safely sheltered from the odd wrath that pummeled the outdoors, the two men wrestled with a dilemma.

CHAPTER 11

August 19, Thursday.

The amber horizon spilled over the deep haze of the mountain range. Nightfall was approaching but still held back by the final life of the day. Miles of fields and wild scenery prepared for nocturnal slumber. But something pierced the looming darkness and the dense layers of misty fog. It was a boy and a crow.

A flurry of footsteps in rapid sequence darted over the plains. Dominic dashed with all of his might as fast as he could. A crow led him in flight through the untamed countryside. His arms and legs pushed forward and backward in perfect harmony. He sprinted desperately to keep up with his guardian.

"Faster!" he shouted to the bird that flew about twenty yards ahead.

Between heavy breaths, Dominic commanded with urgency. "Hurry!"

They hurried together towards a horrific scene that played out in front of them, but they were still quite a distance away. It was Clyde swinging an ax furiously at Mara's heavy, massive trunk. Large pieces of the tree's flesh were violently slashed out from the giant girth with every few strikes from his powerful ax.

He continued his attack with rage with the look of a mad man. His eyes were clamped open with excitement and his teeth were pressed hard against each other; his lips pulled back in a wince as if he was in intense pain and droplets of saliva sprayed in every direction with his frantic motion. But, it was pure satisfaction and victory that possessed him. Victory over the sacred tree. He hated Mara.

As the crow came closer to the chaos and Dominic followed behind, it approached Clyde attacking the tree. Dominic was close enough to see slain crows on the ground spread about the scene. Victims of the evil that wielded his weapon.

Dominic shouted a command with his loudest voice as he sprinted.

"Nooooo! Stop!"

Clyde swung one last time into the steel-like bark, but still no match for the force of the power behind his strength. He breathed heavily with great exertion and quickly turned towards the approaching boy. The crow was first to arrive and, with a mighty force, it descended upon Clyde with its razor-like talons out in attack formation.

"Come here you flying menace!"

Clyde screamed in anticipation of the clash between them. He held the ax back to one side in preparation for another deadly swing.

"I'm ready for you!"

Dominic was close behind the crow as he closed in on Clyde and the tree. Like a bolt of lightning the crow flew at Clyde's head, but within a second, flapped its wings in a downward motion to catch itself just before striking him. The bird immediately pushed away from Clyde just as he used all of his might to swing the long ax at the flying assailant. He missed by mere inches as the crow evaded the swing and the ax swung downward and plunged into the ground. Just then, Dominic reached Clyde and he slid down to his feet and held down the ax with his arms. Without haste, the crow reversed its wing's direction and thrust forward towards the man's face. As Clyde still gripped the handle of the ax with both hands, the black talons aimed for his jugulars and slashed both sides of his neck. As its claws punctured and severed his throat, the crow thrust its sharp beak deep into Clyde's forehead instantly taking his life. The tall figure who committed this act of violent rage against Mara and the crows collapsed backward lifelessly onto the grassy field beneath. The crow detached itself from the corpse and leaped upward to inspect Mara's damage.

Dominic stood and turned to assess the carnage all around him. Every crow was killed, bloodied, and destroyed. Huge chunks of the tree were scattered around the base of the trunk; the debris appeared to be remains of the fury of a tornado that ripped through Mara with ease. Most of its massive trunk had been torn away causing a potentially fatal wound. The last crow was now perched on Mara. Its name was Jasper. Clyde's blood remained on its long beak and its claws. Dominic walked over to it and stood there in sadness over the group of lifeless crows. But it was over. The evil that plagued the land was now gone.

Suddenly, a furious wind blew through a small opening in his bedroom window. It forced some toys and a picture frame that rested on a table to fall on the floor. The loudness abruptly woke Dominic from his deep sleep. He was startled and sat up quickly in his bed. He breathed heavily as if he was running. He sat motionless in his dark bedroom for a moment recalling his dream. *It was a dream*, he thought. It was so vivid and emotionally draining. But only a dream. He was relieved because he cared so much for the crows and Mara.

He slowly climbed out of his bed and walked over to his window. His hands held the bottom rail and pulled the window down to keep the wind from blowing into his room. Right there perched on the outside window frame was his guardian crow. The boy smiled and waved.

"You were in my dream," said Dominic to the crow. "And your name is Jasper."

The bird simply cawed once in acknowledgment.

The early day outside called to him and offered Dominic a day of hope. And hope was exactly what he needed for his mother.

~

His tight, black leather gloves covered his weathered hands as he looked through Samantha's medical chart. With meticulous eyes, he surveyed her latest medical developments and the most recent course of treatment. Clyde was disappointed to learn that she would be having an improved few days according to the doctor's notes. Disappointed that illness had not consumed her by now.

His eyes burned with anger and he began to seethe in his frustration with every passing second. His temples pulsated from his increased heart rate and he put down the chart to clench both fists. Surely there was something he could do. Perhaps something that could alter the current positive course of her health. Even though Clyde was well aware she would meet her end after the next few days, the thought of her dying sooner appealed to him. His devious smile began to form. His fists relaxed and suddenly he had an idea.

~

Dani was behind the wheel to escort Samantha and Dominic on another outing to the country. Since she loved her time spent away from the town earlier that year, Samantha wanted to visit there once again. To think it was only yesterday when she was hospitalized and Dr. Brimmer gave her the bleak news, it was a miracle that she had a renewed strength just as the medical team had said she would. She felt refreshed and strengthened physically. And it was her goal to make the best of her day and the couple of days that followed.

"What a beautiful day we have here, kiddos," said Dani as she turned on the radio. "This is a great idea, Sam. And those delicious sandwiches you helped me make, Dommie, are going to be amazing."

Her upbeat attitude helped the overall mood.

Samantha smiled as she enjoyed the view from the passenger seat.

"Yeah. I'm ready for a good day," she replied.

Dominic smiled proudly. His hoagie-making skills were top-notch for a six-year-old. With Dani's guidance, he was sure to become a master at this craft one day.

Their car swept through the open road as they crossed fields only found in the happiest of dreams. They found a spot in the middle of where nowhere and decided to settle there for a picnic. Dani parked the car but kept the music playing as they unpacked their belongings. Dominic wasted no time and he darted out from the back seat with his kite in hand.

"There he goes," said Samantha. "That boy has so much energy but you couldn't tell from his typical demeanor. I'm glad he's having fun out here."

"How are you feeling?" asked Dani.

"I feel wonderful today," Samantha answered. "This medication is doing exactly what they said it would."

They spread a large blanket over the untamed grassy plain with wildflowers surrounding them in every direction. The distance seemed like forever in its reach with trees displayed in large clusters everywhere they looked. The breeze was mild but carried with it a very cool touch. The warmth of the bright sun countered the chill in the air and made a perfect day for a light jacket. The day was sublime.

Dominic enjoyed his moment with his fun kite. He whimsically danced and hopped across the fields holding his homemade paper aircraft as high in the air as he could. It didn't catch enough wind to propel into the atmosphere, but that didn't matter to him. He aimlessly fled into the wild.

Jasper swooped across the sky so very high above Dominic. Even from a distance, the crow could detect any oncoming threat to the boy from all directions. Its vision was acute, just like that of an intimidating predator. The only evidence of his stealth position was a shadow cast on the plains from the strength of the sun.

Samantha and Dani both rested on the blanket sipping chilled tea and talking about old times when they were younger. Occasionally, they both scanned the area where Dominic played, but they knew he was perfectly safe. The view for miles helped them keep a watchful eye if he wanted to continue his playful journey further away.

The magnificent landscape was attractive to a boy with a big vision. He felt right at home in here and seemed to be drawn to its splendor. It reminded him of the dream with his father. The strong emotions evoked from that connection, although unreal, brought Dominic to hope that he would see his father once again. He searched for Russell in the event he was caught in a dream right then and there. Sometimes you just don't know.

As he continued to hop through the serene terrain, now almost a couple of hundred yards away from his family, he noticed something very familiar. It was a tree just like he saw in his dream the night before. He changed directions and began to jog that way, to the east.

"Do you think we should call him back?" asked Dani.

"Well, as long as we can see him he should be fine. I know we're safe out here in the middle of nowhere," Samantha replied. "Let's give him a few more minutes before we do anything. He's enjoying himself."

"It looks like he's heading for that huge tree now," said Dani.

Dominic approached Mara with great anticipation. He knew this was a sacred place. He was close enough now to see a group of crows that huddled within beneath its outstretched limbs in all directions. His eyes widened at its enormous size, towering height, and width. He had never seen anything so large in his young life. Suddenly, from out of the sky, Jasper descended and landed on one of Mara's lower branches. Dominic stopped as he reached the trunk and recognized his protector.

"Hey, you followed me here?" said Dominic to the bird.

The crow cawed as if it was replying to the boy.

Dominic was so amazed at how massive the tree's branches extended over him. It easily blocked out the daylight in a large area all around him. It felt as though he was surrounded by a gigantic cloud. He was secure and comforted by Mara and these amazing guardians.

The battalion of crows did not feel threatened and they knew Dominic had no ill intentions towards Mara. Their allegiance to the sacred tree was pure, but they also could sense a true threat. This boy was an ally, not a danger to them at all.

He began to speak to Mara. His innocent mind and creative spirit supported a belief in this tree's purpose. A childlike mind is what allows people this freedom and to not be swayed by life's cares.

"Hi, Mara. I'm Dominic."

Almost as sure as an audible voice from his mother, Dominic was able to hear Mara's reply. He was puzzled but also intrigued at this sense he had. Because it was obvious that people cannot talk to inanimate objects, animals, or organic life such as trees. It was impossible. And yet here he was able to hear thoughts and words from Mara in a personal conversation.

"I know who you are, Dominic," said Mara. "You are highly regarded and have a wonderful future ahead of you. I know this because of your mother, Samantha. She has tasted the sacred nectar of my fruit and so have you. She has traded her life to give you yours."

He understood everything he was told and was surprised a tree could know his family's circumstances. He continued with their conversation.

"She's sick now. I'm sad because she won't be with me anymore. Just like my Daddy."

He looked towards the horizon over his left shoulder with a somber gaze. Before Mara could reply he heard a very familiar voice calling to him.

"Dommie. Are you okay?" Samantha shouted from an open window of the car.

Dani drove her because Samantha was in no condition to jog over to where he was. The car pulled up alongside Dominic who stood beside Mara.

"What are you doing here?"

"Mommy, this is the tree," he answered. "This is the tree in my dream. I found it."

"Okay, honey. I understand, but can we go now?" she asked. "Let's drive you back to our picnic area."

She curiously looked at the formation of crows within the massive tree.

"Why do these birds continue to show up?"

"They're protectors," Dominic said. "Protectors of this tree. And the one right there is my crow. He follows me everywhere."

He pointed to Jasper before he opened the rear passenger door and jumped in. Although all of the crows had the same appearance, except for Chancellor, Dominic could distinguish them from each other. His gift was developing.

Samantha and Dani looked at each other for a moment, still trying to comprehend the matter. They grinned slightly at each other but made sure he didn't notice them in the front seat. They knew Dominic had a wide imagination and could reach deep within his creative basin for such stories.

But then Samantha became immediately entranced by Mara. She paused and stared intently at the tree and suddenly a voice spoke to her in her mind. Words from no one else before, yet they were strangely familiar and soothing. Dani didn't interrupt Samantha. She sensed something was going on inside of her.

"It's nice to meet you, Samantha," said Mara. "I've been waiting for this moment for a while."

Samantha stood puzzled and wasn't sure what to think. She just listened and said nothing in return. The tree continued to speak to her mind.

"We are keeping watch over Dominic. Know that he is safe. Stay well and fight against this evil that has stricken your health. Your day is coming."

She frowned and processed those words. At first, she couldn't understand why she could hear this tree talk to her. Samantha looked at Mara's trunk, massive limbs outstretched in every direction, and the gathering of many crows within the belly of this tree as if she was inspecting it. Then slowly she accepted the truth and smiled. A reassurance swept over her. A calm and peace like nothing else before captured her heart. She didn't respond but somehow knew this would not be the last time they would interact.

"Hey, Sam," said Dani as she gently touched Samantha's shoulder. "Let's eat some lunch."

"Uh, yeah," said Samantha. She looked at Dani and agreed.

"You okay?" Dani asked.

"Yeah. I'm perfect," said Samantha.

Dominic stared out of his window and waved to the tree and the crows as the car retreated into the wilderness. They resumed their family picnic and did not discuss the tree or the crows for the rest of that day. Instead, they enjoyed a satisfying lunch and light-hearted conversation. Dominic stood close by and played with the toys that he brought from home. Every so often, he peeked into the open blue sky in search of his crow. But he couldn't see any birds other than the robins that flew overhead every so often. He wondered if his guardian was watching over him from a nearby tree. Then he convinced himself it was so. A guardian so great as his would never leave him.

They remained out in their excursion for just a little while longer and decided to bring Samantha back home at an early hour. She was feeling this new strength, but she was not completely well either. And Dani did not want her best friend to overextend herself.

~

The cool of the evening began to settle and chill their bodies. Dani and Samantha huddled around a warm fire in her backyard. The glowing blaze lulled them both into a sense of calm and peace. As they sipped hot tea and enjoyed the comfort a thought penetrated Samantha's mind.

"Hey, Dani. Did we get today's mail?" she asked. "There's a document I'm waiting for from the insurance company. I should've received it by now."

"No, but I'll check now," Dani said as she quickly stood and walked back into the house.

After a couple of minutes, she returned holding a few pieces of mail that arrived that day. She returned to her chair and handed them to Samantha.

The soft glow of the fire was bright enough to read her mail, even under the early darkness of the evening. She sifted through the envelopes until she noticed one in particular that caught her attention.

"Whoa. Look at this!" she said to Dani.

Her friend curiously leaned over to see what it was.

"Nice envelope. Is someone we know getting married?" Samantha said as she turned it over to see who it was from, but there was no name or address other than hers.

"No," said Dani.

Samantha ignored the other documents and set them down at her feet with one hand while she studied the ivory embellished envelope. It contained something of great value because of the weight of its contents and there was a ruby-colored, wax seal that covered the flap. The seal was very thin and Samantha gently rubbed her fingers over it for a moment admiring the care someone took with this card. Especially the shiny gold lettering used for her name and address. It was very elegant.

"Hurry up and open it!" said Dani. "The suspense is annoying me! Who's it from?"

"There's no return address or name, other than my own," said Samantha.

Samantha was like a giddy child in a candy store. She held the envelope to one side as she separated the flap and the underside of the envelope with her pinky finger. Slowly and carefully, she pulled, separated, and broke the seal. The flap and the seal still intact opened upward revealing a shiny gold card inside.

144

"Oooh, pretty!" Samantha said with a surprised look.

She removed the gold card from the envelope and handed the outer covering to Dani as she then took a long gaze at the front of this beautiful and ornate card. The front was lined in deep ivory inlays and raised in areas that had a design. After a moment, she realized the design was a form of an open palm and fingers outstretched. It resembled a gesture of someone offering to take their hand. She touched the raised and inlay formations with her right hand as if to receive this offering.

"Go on!" Dani blurted out.

Samantha took the bottom corner and opened the card to reveal the inside. A pearly gloss was the first thing she noticed. The background was of royal flair and in the center, there were the following words written in calligraphy, by hand. It read:

Dearest Samantha,
You are cordially invited to attend my 33rd birthday celebration on
August 21. I will notify you of the specific time and place.
Sincerely,
Julius C.

Her mouth opened and her eyes welled up with fresh tears. Samantha was in shock as Dani took the card from her hand and began to sob after reading the handwritten note. They turned to each other with amazement and could not believe this was happening.

"Does this mean you will… Wait, is this a wish transfer, Samantha?" Dani asked eagerly.

Samantha nodded her head and her eyes closed with teardrops streaming down both of her cheeks.

"Yes," she replied. "Yes, it is."

She immediately felt the soothing relief come over her heart. The comfort and satisfying heat put forth from the cozy fire was paled by comparison to how she felt. This new peace overshadowed any grief or sorrow she had been wrestling with. She could sense her life being lifted from out of the caverns of despair and placed into the high mountains of security. It was sanctuary. It was perfect hope.

They leaned into each other, embraced, and laughed in celebration. This was a moment of victory on the horizon. And suddenly there was a pause by Samantha as she pulled away.

"Wait. I don't know how many others were also invited." Samantha said, now abruptly confused. "There could be a few people or a very large gathering. I remember for my birthday I was able to invite as many potential recipients as I wanted. But, I chose Dommie. Julius knows so many people and comes into contact with a large number of Stillwhorm patients. Why would he bother with inviting me?"

The sudden reality dashed the sparks that were there moments earlier. It felt as though a gift was opened and the box was empty. They hesitated for a while before speaking. The wind had now escaped their sails. Now a part of her began to resent Julius for even sending this invitation.

Samantha broke the quiet air between them.

"I have to remain hopeful and positive. I must remind myself this was my decision. I gave my life to my son on purpose. I transferred that hope into his life. I shouldn't act like this. I need to be grounded for the next couple of days. My last couple of days."

"Hey, you don't have to say anything to me, Sam," Dani replied. "I was right there with you, practically jumping for joy."

Thirty-three Crows

Quietly in his room, Dominic was coloring. He allowed his heart to guide his markers on the empty paper. The shape of his drawing was becoming clear. It was a large yellow birthday cake with purple edges and in the shape of an oval. He wasn't alone. Even though his window was closed he could sense Jasper watching over him.

Dominic admired the drawing and picked up a new color marker. In deep crimson red, he drew on the cake the number "33." He smiled, filled with satisfaction, and looked over his shoulder at the crow.

"Thank you for being here," he said.

CHAPTER 12

August 20, Friday

The next morning, Samantha woke up feeling drained. It was just enough to remember that her time remained was brief. She remembered what Dr. Brimmer had told her upon discharge the day before last. She would require additional fluids at some point and that was a side effect of the medication they introduced. Although she had so much new energy, it was the morning's exhaustion that caused her to prepare for a visit to the medical center.

Samantha made her morning tea and told Dani, who was preparing breakfast for them, that she would be back in a couple of hours. She kissed Dominic and told him she would return. After grabbing her tea in a travel mug and a slice of toast, Samantha grabbed her purse and headed out the door.

The receptionist greeted her when she walked into the center.

"Good morning, Samantha. How are you feeling?"

"Oh, I'm doing much better than before," she answered. "I just need some fluids this morning."

"Come on back and Robin will take you to a room," the smiling staff member said.

"Thanks," Samantha said as she walked back into the triage area and met Robin.

"Hi, Samantha. Let's take you back and get you out of here quickly," said Robin.

Samantha made herself comfortable in a large sofa chair used in the infusion area. These were used for short-term, IV administered treatments. The room was bright and had four of these large chairs in every corner, separated by a pull curtain. But there were no other patients in the room Samantha was escorted to.

Robin called down to the floor's supply pharmacy for Samantha's bag of saline. Five minutes later, the IV fluid was delivered to the nurse's station. She brought it along with a package of tubing. Robin noticed that the bag felt slightly warmer than the typical room temperature bags she handles daily. But the label fixed to the bag showed that it was a new mixture and did not seem like a problem.

"Alright. Let's get you going," Robin said while priming the tubing and loading it into the pump.

She put on sterile gloves before prepping her port for the needle.

"Okay, small pinch."

The nurse was gentle and had veteran hands from years of service to the patients who came in for health care.

"What's this, Robin?" Samantha asked as the nurse set the rate and commenced the infusion.

"Standard D10 solution with some electrolytes," said Robin as she removed her gloves and picked up the pieces of alcohol wipe packages. Then she realized Samantha was puzzled.

"Sorry. D10 is a saline solution with 10% dextrose. It's very common for us to use this to support the body with hydration.

You'll only have an hour and a half on this machine before you're done."

Robin smiled and asked if she needed anything.

Samantha thanked her and said she was fine. As the nurse left the room, Samantha nestled into the comfortable lounge chair and focused on the day ahead. She believed it would be a wonderful day with her loved ones once she was done with her infusion. Those thoughts pushed back against the dread of her looming death. She knew with confidence that she had about forty-eight hours of strength that remained. She wanted to make the precious hours count.

She closed her eyes and only heard the melodic sound of the medical pump. The soft mechanical whines lulled her to sleep. It was a lullaby sung to her by rhythmic cycles from a cold machine. It was ironic.

Samantha fell into a deep sleep and after only a few seconds her eyes opened abruptly to behold her beautiful garden. She stood there amid radiant sunshine and elegant flowers as far as the eye could see in every direction, except to the north. In that direction, a formidable stance of dense pine trees stood like giants and formed a massive wall of dread. Wicked darkness was contained within and fear seeped from the outskirts of this intimidating fortress. She told herself to stay away from that place.

She glanced to her left then to her right. *This couldn't be happening* she thought. All she could remember was sitting in her chair receiving her infusion, just moments before. Suddenly she found herself plucked out of the medical center and placed into this interesting scene. She stood there amazed and confused.

Her bare feet took small steps forward as she continued to assess her new surroundings. Then she heard a rustling coming from the trees ahead of her. It sounded like leaves and sticks being crushed by footsteps. She focused on the direction from where the sound came from and her eyes pinpointed the very source. It was a tall figure walking within the dense layers of the forest. It moved towards her in large strides through a fog-like covering. She suddenly recognized the individual. It was Clyde.

He continued to walk with a steady cadence towards her. His heavy footsteps crumbled foliage beneath his towering presence until he reached the perimeter of the woods. As the sunlight illuminated his body once he walked out of the cover of darkness, she could see his formal appearance. Clyde was well dressed in a black pinstriped suit, burgundy bow tie, and a black, wide-brimmed fedora. He spoke to Samantha as he approached and made distinct eye contact with her. He was spellbound.

"Hello, Samantha. It's so good to see you."

His voice pierced her heart with a sense of bitterness and shock. She suddenly felt a shortness of breath in her lungs; she gasped and struggled to breathe. It was obvious to her that his presence meant something evil was about to take place, but she was also frozen with curiosity.

"Allow me a few moments of your time," he said. "Please don't walk away, Samantha."

"Why am I here?" she asked. "And where am I?"

"Well, you're in a place within a dream. I've brought you to a location where you can find sanctuary. Do you trust me?" he asked.

"I'm not sure how I got here, but I've got to return to the medical center."

Samantha answered with a sense of urgency and panic.

"I don't have much time left," she said frantically.

Those last few words brought a grin to Clyde's demeanor. The edges of his mouth were now upturned as he was delighted with her predicament.

"I know, Samantha. Time is your most precious thing."

He now stopped within an arm's distance from Samantha. His towering height was imposing. He clasped his hands in front of him then slowly and deliberately rested them down in front of his waist.

"I want to offer you peace this very moment. Would you like that?"

"I'm so tired," her voice trembled with emotion. "Peace, yes. I want this nightmare to be over."

"Just take my hand," he said as he stretched out his arm to her. "All you have to do is join me and I will escort you to a place you have never seen before. It is time to leave behind the hurts and the disappointments of your life. Russell and Dominic have caused you an immense amount of heartache and sorrow."

Samantha closed her eyes and reached out her right hand to take his. His offer was soothing and she believed what he said. He took her by the hand and gently turned himself around to lead his victim back into the imprisonment of the woods.

"Come with me," he said.

As her eyes were closed she became caught in his trance. They slowly walked hand in hand several steps through the beautiful garden and into the heavy darkness within the dense woods. Coldness breached her warm skin and infiltrated beneath her tissues. A heavy layer of mist surrounded them and their footsteps echoed between the staggering heights of the trees.

"She's coding!"

Robin shouted to the rest of the team on the floor. A pulsating alarm screamed throughout the floor. Its emergent sound meant someone was dying. And that someone was Samantha who was convulsing in her chair and didn't respond to the nurse's questions.

Dr. Brimmer and two other medical staff immediately rushed to the room to render aid. Samantha's body shook and then quickly became motionless. They stopped the infusion and gave her a shot of Miquelten to combat the Stillwhorm attack, or so they thought that was what caused the violent reaction. Her breathing continued, but she was still unresponsive. Samantha seemed to be caught in a state of comatose.

Through the dense chill of the covering between the eerie pines deep within her dream, Clyde eased Samantha towards a destination of his choosing. A place where he would set her free from her mortal existence and usher her into the afterlife. He let go of her hand and placed his arm securely around her shoulders as they walked slowly. He took smaller steps to keep pace with her cadence. At last, his desire to destroy her life was about to be fulfilled.

"You've suffered long enough," he began to coax her mind with manipulation. "I've waiting patiently for years to help you through these final moments."

They continued to move forward through the vast, misty darkness one intentional step at a time. It was as if he was walking her down the aisle before giving her hand away in marriage—with death. Ahead of them, there was a specific destination prepared just for her; a gravesite with a personalized headstone. It read:

SAMANTHA PARSONS
FROM BIRTH TO DEATH
BY THE HAND OF STILLWHORM SYNDROME

Clyde wanted to be the one to bury her cold corpse into his turf. These were his terms and he was about to fulfill his mission.

153

Samantha felt the heaviness of his spell now and she had no power over his deception.

The sinister one envisioned this moment for decades. The appetite for Samantha's destruction was about to be quenched and her doom was imminent. He could almost taste his victory.

He continued to speak and give his identity away knowing she was about to perish forever.

"It's a shame that you didn't know who I was from the moment we first met. A member of the Office of State? No. I am the poisonous and the treacherous disease itself; I AM Stillwhorm Syndrome. Many have fallen by my hand including your sweet Russell."

Samantha now firmly entranced in his web, was powerless and also able to comprehend his confession. The heart that broke from the blow of her husband's death now raced beneath her chest. It pumped blood faster by the force of squirts of adrenaline as she heard his every word. The news upset her tremendously. Yet, her eyes remained closed and her motion continued forward with her captor.

"Did you know that it was by my hand that your parents were killed as well? I unleashed every ounce of terror upon them. They had poured everything good of themselves into you. I punished them severely for making you nearly impenetrable with their uttered words—their protective spoken coverings."

Clyde became bitter and angst rose from his lips.

"I hated them. They cursed my attempts to gather you with my arms and poison you. For as long as they petitioned for your security and hopeful future I had no power over you. Do you see what they've done, Samantha?"

Rage began to spew from him and his eyes scowled like a madman. Samantha had no way to speak or open her eyes now. It was like a deep sleep she could not awaken from, but deep down she trembled with anger and comprehension. It was a perfect nightmare.

Their procession through the thick atmosphere of despair continued. Bitter cold and heavy moisture in the air caused shivers to run throughout her body. Doom and dread surrounded her and she could hear faint, devious laughter from every direction.

"They deserved every bit of punishment I unleashed upon them. And they suffered tremendously. Do you understand now? They stood in my way!"

His anger overwhelmed him. He stopped short of the gravesite and conceded to his wrath. He let out unrestrained wicked howls and yelling as he raised his eyes upward. His screams shook the air with shockwaves and echoed through the vast imprisonment of trees. If any living creatures scurried about they would be terrified by the sounds of his terrible agony.

Suddenly, an unannounced boom cracked through the skies. The sound shocked Clyde and strangely struck terror in his heart. It was as if the heavens parted with a powerful sonic resonance. Within a split second, from out of nowhere, something forceful struck him like a bolt of lightning and it pummeled him onto his back. His lanky body fell hard against the ground and before he knew what happened the attack continued. Another immediate strike caused lacerations deep into his neck. He clenched his severed throat with both hands and screamed out in fear as blood seeped through his fingers. More blinding strikes ripped across his eyebrow nearly tearing his face in half and across his chest that penetrated his clothing slashing his flesh. With each furious blow inflicted with superior speed, he cried out in anger and shock. The pain was so intense that it caused him stifling torment. It thwarted his attempt to carry out his death sentence upon Samantha.

As the attack unfolded, a band of crows came to her rescue. Samantha stood paralyzed as Clyde remained on his back, in overwhelming shock. In one fluid movement, the crows took hold of Samantha and flapped their wings. Her body fell lifeless in their grasp as she floated upwards into a vertical ascent. Their incredible power elevated Samantha up through the trees as her assailant diminished below the murky mist of the woods. She was set free.

Motionless on his back, he quickly scanned his surroundings to find his attacker. It was Chancellor, the mighty crow that now hovered over him in flight. Clyde was stunned by the fierce attack and he looked around for his victim, but she was gone. Angered and bloodied, he cried out with uncontrollable hostility at Chancellor and quickly managed to rise to his feet. It was just him and the fierce crow, face to face. Chancellor floated with ease above its prey by the power of its mighty wings and in attack formation. Clyde breathed in and out heavily from the shock and, still deeply dazed, he continued to look around for Samantha. His severe neck wounds poured blood onto his suit and his eyes now held a look of panic. He was a madman in distress.

"What did you do? We're in her dream."

He said with a growling voice filled with rising hatred. His tongue curled as he gurgled blood deep in his throat.

"Where is she?"

With one loud shriek, Chancellor rapidly shot up into the air high above the treetops like a blazing missile because he knew Samantha was now safe and it had to return to Mara. Its wings were so massive and strong, they caused the dense forest to sway behind it in its powerful departure and the foggy layers to swirl below. They were able to propel the crow at tremendous speeds and cause atmosphere blasts and rumblings with its sheer force.

Clyde turned and started to run back to the garden in hopes he would find her there helplessly in his trance. He staggered and fell continuously, stunned by his assailant. His moans of anger and pain were trapped beneath the imposing pines.

His pursuit had failed. He tasted defeat by the hand of his arch-enemy. Clyde's pride clouded his reality to the extent that he had forgotten the power of Mara's crows. They could enter his reality, whether within a dream or in the physical realm, and bring the fight to him on any ground. They rescued Samantha from his imprisonment and she was safely escorted out of the peril of her dream.

He fell once more and was exhausted as he laid against the coldness of the dirt and gravel. His breathing was shallow and unstable. Clyde had never felt this intense pain before. He picked up his head slowly and turned his chin upward to the sky.

"Nooooo!"

He moaned into the moist darkness.

Samantha soared above the treetops and across the brightly lit sky carried by a group of guardian crows. Each one gripped her securely for a safe passage. She was unconscious and still under the spell of Clyde's poison. But her rescue was successful.

Familiar sounds echoed in her mind, then voices calling her name were heard back at the medical facility. She started to wake from her sleep and whisper incoherent mumbling. Samantha looked at the team of doctors and nurses standing around her. Confused and scared, her eyes shifted around quickly to find that menace of evil. But Clyde was not there.

"Samantha? Can you hear me?" asked Dr. Brimmer.

His look of panic and concern was alarming to Samantha as well as the sudden new team of faces that huddled over her. He looked at Samantha and smiled with immediate relief.

"Well, that was scary. You had a terrible reaction to something. But you're safe now."

She tried to raise her head forward from the reclined chair. Her head felt as if it was restrained and dizzy. She moaned with discomfort before she spoke quietly.

"I feel terrible. My lungs…ribs…pain. My head…killing me," she said.

She held her head and shook it in disbelief. Her eyes squinted as her vision was blurry and her speech was impaired from the agony.

"What happened? Mom. Dad," she said as she crumbled under intense sobbing. "Russ."

She recollected what Clyde revealed about her parents and her husband. The emotional shock alarmed her.

"Your body was severely attacked and we found you convulsing here just after your hydration run began. We immediately stopped running the D10 solution and gave you a shot to quickly boost your immunity. It worked. But I'm afraid something deeper is going on," said Dr. Brimmer as he sat beside her.

"We'll call Dani and Robin will move you into another room. With this new episode, I'm not sure how much time we have. It might be a matter of hours," he said.

"Dommie," Samantha whispered under her crying with a blank stare. "Dommie."

The trap was successful. Set by Clyde before Samantha's hydration run, he breathed his poison into the bag of D10 saline as it was mixed with electrolytes by the medical center's pharmacist. He knew she would need this infusion the very next morning because Dr. Brimmer told her so. So he waited as patiently as he could for Robin to send that order down for the bag. It was a perfect idea and was meant to bring about her rapid decline towards her death. Until her rescue shattered his plan.

She was relocated to a treatment area and Dani rushed to see her with Dominic. They gathered themselves with her in the private room. They tried to lift her spirits in her weakened state. But it was her spirit itself that was shattered. She often stared at the clock hanging across from her bed wondering how many breaths she had remaining.

Then two more familiar faces appeared. Frank and Naomi tapped on the door as they stepped into her room. Their bright faces brought another layer of comfort.

"Hi there," Frank said gently.

"Hi," Naomi added. "Robin called us."

Samantha was pleased to see their kind faces. It reminded her of the recent moments shared with the CU team. But someone was missing.

"Where's Julius?" she asked in a wheezing exhale as her labored breathing was obvious that her body was breaking down.

"He took some personal time off this week. He said he had some things to prepare for," said Frank.

Samantha thought about the invitation she had received from Julius. Then she realized in her haze that his birthday celebration was near. It was tomorrow. Somehow she managed to believe there was a speck of hope that remained. It was tucked away safely deep within the corner of her heart. She decided to pluck it, like a dazzling flower from her spectacular garden, and hold it out as a beacon that casts away all fear.

She looked around her room for her son and extended her arms to Dominic once she found him. He climbed up into her bed and kissed her cheek. She held him with the last of her strength; her weakened body was almost lifeless.

The room was filled with love. The love between a mother and her son; between best friends and new friends unified by acts of service. And love was the only thing that could envelop Samantha right then and there. Pure and powerful love.

~

Clyde sat motionless in a dark cavern, his lair within the deathly woods. He was gravely injured and he tried to assess and mend himself, just as a wild animal licks its wounds after the battle. The defeat he encountered disturbed him deeply. His pride was shattered beneath his once stiff arrogance. And the deep gashes across his neck and face—the grotesque carnage caused by the crow—were painful reminders of his loss.

The uncomfortable granite floor he rested on didn't bother him at all. He was still focused on destroying Samantha's legacy and ending any hope that would derive from her or her son's future actions. He closed his eyes and allowed the fury to rise. The single candle barely illuminated his cold surroundings and its small flame didn't flicker because the air was deathly still.

His presence in solitude was proof that he had no power anywhere else for that moment. Something happened from his attack by Chancellor. Something was different in his body. An unusual warmth filled his bloodstream and it was foreign to him. A presence he had never felt within. *What could this be?* He thought and contemplated the possibilities.

Perhaps it was a strike from Chancellor's claws armed with a venom that invaded his body. Maybe with each slash from its black talons, a toxin was introduced to take his life. He couldn't understand what it was, but he knew he was fading away. There was no way for him to extract the toxin from his body. It was just as deadly as the very poison he inflicted to cause Stillwhorm Syndrome in the land.

160

Suddenly, he understood firsthand the despair his victims experienced as they fell under his venomous bite. It was foreign territory for Clyde. He became so accustomed to his role as the predator that, now as a victim, he panicked with his fate. His wiry figure slumped down to the ground, groggy from his circumstance. His life was fading.

Weakened and frail, he lifted his trembling hand to his neck. With his long ashy fingers, he touched the open gashes still fresh from Chancellor. The tip of his index finger eased across the length of the wound and he dipped it into his flesh. He winced and held his breath as the pain shot through his entire body. Then, he took that finger and raised it to his lips. The taste of his blood mingled with an undeniable sourness proved his suspicions were correct. It was the Cura fruit from Mara. Poison from his enemy. He screamed with every fiber of his being. A roar that carried through the empty caverns and fell onto no one's ears. Anger and rage consumed his end.

Yes, it was Mara's sacred fruit that was thrust into his flesh by Chancellor. Before the crows were dispatched for Samantha's rescue, Mara instructed Chancellor to puncture its long talons and beak into one of the most potent fruits that hung from a particular branch. The crow obeyed and flew to the precise area where it hung. It primed its long beak first with repeated jabs then ripped a small portion of the Cura to hold as well. Then it pierced each one of its black talons deep within the fruit's mass and saturated its claws.

Clyde knew he didn't have much time. He could barely sit hunched over and he began to gasp for his last breaths of air; these were his final moments. Mara had poisoned him to completely expel his vengeance from Esid Arapym. The pain was excruciating throughout his limbs and his body. He began coughing violently as sharp jolts punished his lungs. The torture was unbearable.

His shallow breathing became heavy wheezing. Clyde suffered through his final breaths of air. Lifeless, he crumbled completely to the cold ground. He could not muster the power to return to his normal state of a spirit-likeness. No, he would breathe his last in his mortal fleshly form. Anger spewed from his weak heart as defeat was accepted.

"I've failed," the sinister one whispered and gurgled in a well of blood from his throat. "I release you."

Then with his final exhale, Clyde Serwhoven's reign of terror came to an end. He was defeated by the power of good. His corpse remained there until the Killworm was summoned to cleanse the land from his decay. And in the distance, a thunderous rumble shook the earth. Rage was expelled from below.

~

Dr. Brimmer walked into her room holding her chart under his left arm. He held a cup of coffee with his right and had a concerned look on his face. This proved to be the most difficult day for Samantha and his team.

"How you holding up?" he asked Samantha.

She moved her head slowly from side to side to respond. A strange paleness had now replaced her vibrant and healthy skin. And her eyes were gaunt and distressed. Samantha was too frail to speak. It was now the afternoon and about eight hours since her episode earlier that day. Her strength was failing and Dr. Brimmer did everything he could to keep her alert and alive.

Dani sat with Dominic at her lap bedside. Frank and Naomi remained there as well. They both sat in chairs across from Samantha's bed. They each took turns to leave and bring back food and drinks for Dani and Dominic. Their support was priceless.

The doctor checked her pulse after he set down his coffee and gently felt her head with his hand. His voice was filled with compassion as he leaned over slightly and spoke just above a whisper.

"I'm so sorry. I'm doing everything I can for you."

His voice was calming.

"Keep fighting, Samantha."

He stood and turned to Dani and Dominic.

"How are you both holding up?"

"We're okay," said Dani.

He smiled and nodded. Then began to explain the situation.

"I can't give her anymore Miquelten. It will only do more damage. We'll continue to administer a steady infusion of fluids at a slow rate and a periodic steroid dose to maintain her strength for now. But pain management is our highest priority."

"I understand. Thank you, doctor," replied Dani.

He stepped out after picking up his Styrofoam cup. Samantha turned toward Dominic who climbed on the edge of her bed. She slowly raised her hand to touch his face. Her gloomy eyes looked at him with such love that words were not necessary. And he understood completely.

Periodically, Robin and another nurse, Sherry, checked on Samantha, her infusion levels, and her guests. They paid close attention to her appearance and vitals. It was apparent to the medical team that she was in her final hours. They kept her very comfortable.

The final attack from Clyde proved to be the last blow she could endure. His poison infiltrated her entire bloodstream and her tissues. Although she did not perish upon his final urging in the woods, it was certain that Stillwhorm Syndrome had claimed an early victory over Samantha. Her finality was looming.

As the evening was upon them, Frank and Naomi offered one last run for anything they needed before leaving. Visiting hours were over except for close family. Dani was an exception since Samantha had no family other than Dominic. Dani declined their offer and said goodbye to them.

"We'll be back in the morning," said Frank.

Then he turned to Samantha with a gracious smile.

"Stay strong."

Naomi approached her bed and placed her hand on Samantha's. She did not speak but instead looked upon her friend with grace and love. Her unspoken gesture was conveyed by her eyes and Samantha received her expression of such friendship. Frank and Naomi's presence warmed her heart.

Frank took Naomi's hand, and they left the room.

Dani dimmed the lights for a more comfortable setting. She prepared the sofa at the back of the room for Dominic to sleep. Earlier, the nurse brought sheets, blankets, and pillows for them to remain with Samantha.

Once he was laid down to rest, Dani went back to Samantha's side and sat with her for a long while. The soft glow of the dimly lit room eased them all into a peaceful night. Samantha fell asleep and Dani stood and watched her. It was probably their final hours together. And Dani hoped for her dear friend to stay with them for at least one more day. She leaned in close to Samantha and moved her hair from the side of her face. She took the blanket with both hands and pulled it up to Samantha's neck.

She whispered to her best friend.

"Samantha. You need to stay with us for just one more day. Please, fight. Fight for your chance tomorrow."

Dani's tears emerged as she quietly urged her friend. Then she pulled the birthday celebration invitation from Julius out of her purse and set it on her friend's chest as she slept.

"Julius offered you hope. Regardless of how many others are there, you need to be there too."

She broke down and sobbed as softly as she could. Between her sobbing, she encouraged her friend.

"You need a wish transfer. Hold on, please."

The room was filled with despair and a somberness from the coldness of near death. Samantha struggled physically to remain alive. Stillwhorm Syndrome overwhelmed her once vibrant life and replaced it with desperation. There was nothing else the team could offer or do to make things better for her. No solutions were available, even as brilliant and as experienced as Dr. Brimmer was in his quest to combat this illness in his patients. Unfortunately, she was about to die.

Dani fell asleep in her chair next to the bed and she was hunched over on Samantha's lap. Robin came in to check on them. She covered Dani with a blanket and made sure she did not wake her. She checked the infusion fluid levels and Samantha's vitals. All was as well as could be. Samantha was stable and holding on to life. She continued to breathe on her own with sufficient oxygen saturation levels. But the worst would begin to pummel her very soon. With utmost certainty, she only had less than a day remaining to live. Maybe only a handful of desperate hours.

CHAPTER 13

August 21, Saturday

It was Saturday. The morning of a new day unfolded its arms to embrace the new events ready to take form. A day of sure doom for a mother who struggled with the end stages of Stillwhorm Syndrome and a day for those who loved her dearly would watch Samantha take her final breaths.

Yet across the downtown pre-dawn bustle, a man contemplated his actions. The cool morning air graced the warm cheeks of Julius as he walked through a grassy field. The new day spilled light across the horizon to chase out the night skies. He spent the early morning hours in deep thought for this special day. He wrestled with his decision and he wondered if there was any other way. But there was not.

His purpose was perfect. His unpenetrated will was intact. He gazed into the skies as they were adorned with fresh colors of bright pink and orange along the undersides of scattered billowy clouds. The background of a deep purple and blue atmosphere still displayed a small collection of sparkling stars that remained from the evening slumber. He was pleased with how beautiful this day began. It marked the ending and the beginning of two lives.

Julius knew what had to be done. It was time. No opposition existed and nothing that could be formed against his act was powerful enough to stammer his purpose. He stepped into his future with boldness.

~

The medical center was quiet as the morning routines began a small shuffling of nurses and other staff around the floor. The hallway that once was asleep with activity began to awaken by the team of nurses that moved with urgency throughout the wing. The slumber of the night fell victim to a new day that held out hope to the patients. Hope was waiting there for Samantha as well.

Dani's eyes peered open as Robin hung a fresh bag of fluids and primed the tubing. The lights were still off, but the night light was enough for the skilled nurse to perform her tasks. Dani sat up in her chair and rubbed her back with both hands. The position she fell asleep in was not the most comfortable, but there was nowhere else she would have been. She glanced over at Samantha who was already awake. They met eyes and exchanged smiles.

"Good morning, you ray of sunshine," Dani said.

"Hello," Samantha replied coarsely with soreness in her throat.

"How are you?" asked Dani.

"Okay, I guess. Hurts to talk," Samantha held her hand to her throat. "But I'm still here."

"Don't. Rest your voice," said Dani.

Samantha looked over to where Dominic had slept through the night peacefully. He was still and curled up in a blanket. The exhaustion from the previous day's events caused him to remain in a deep sleep.

"How is he?" Samantha asked.

"He's holding up well, considering. Busy with his coloring book and had a good dinner."

She smiled and felt the blessing of having her son and her best friend with her. But a new painful headache punished her in throbbing waves. It was a fever that began to overcome her. Her body was breaking down.

Robin also brought with her increased doses of pain meds to help keep her patient as comfortable as possible. This new fever marked a typical symptom that usually commenced a sharp decline in Stillwhorm patients. What followed was a sudden loss of vision followed by internal organ failure and then sudden death.

Dr. Brimmer tapped on the door and peeked his head inside. "Good morning."

He stepped in with a fresh smile and he held a beautiful bouquet of wildflowers for her.

"These are a gift from a friend. He said you would love this arrangement."

Samantha recognized the colorful gathering of floral beauty. The bouquet was unmistakably familiar. These were picked from her garden where she spent countless days tending and caring for the floral collection she had grown since Russell had departed.

"Beautiful," she whispered with a smile as she held out her hands to receive the gift.

The doctor handed them to her and she brought them up to her face as she inhaled their sweet aroma.

"Who did this?" She asked Dr. Brimmer in her coarse voice. Her eyes frowned from the pain in her head and throat.

"They're from Julius," he answered.

Her face grinned with a sense of endearment. Her eyes sparkled as she spoke.

"Today. His birthday."

Dr. Brimmer nodded.

"And we have to get you ready for his celebration," said the doctor. "We don't have much time."

He turned to Robin and asked for several preparations on her behalf. Shift change had already come and gone, but Robin insisted to remain on longer and care for Samantha. The nurse turned and briskly walked out of the room to fulfill his orders. He looked back at Samantha.

"Julius decided to gather here at our conference room because you're in no condition to be moved."

She slowly turned to Dani and expressed a glow of happiness.

"Wish you could be there," said Samantha to her friend then coughed. "I'm a mess."

Dani reassured her.

"Listen, you don't worry about a thing. I'll fix you right up."

"It's not much, but we have a very nice robe for you to wear," said Dr. Brimmer. "When you're ready, Robin will take you down in a wheelchair. Julius would like to commence as soon as you're ready. He's already informed everyone involved."

"Well, let's get this show on the road, girl," said Dani with an upbeat tone. "Doctor, just give us some privacy as I transform Sam into a princess."

"Sure," said Dr. Brimmer. "Oh, and Robin will be right back. I asked her to give you a dose of a pain medication that will help you during the next hour. See you later."

Dr. Brimmer walked out and closed the door behind him.

Dani wasted no time as she grabbed her purse to retrieve makeup and a hairbrush. She began to brighten up Samantha for this special occasion. With all the commotion, Dominic began to wake from his sleep.

"Good morning, Mommy," he said as he walked over and gave her a big hug.

"Good morning. I'm going somewhere. Stay with Dani. Alright?" said Samantha. She kissed her son on his cheek and looked lovingly into his eyes.

The news of Julius' birthday celebration buzzed through the entire facility. This had never happened before. The staff was energized with the excitement. Robin returned with a reclining wheelchair and some other things the doctor had asked for. The ceremony was specific with its parameters and guidelines. The Council made sure all adherences were followed strictly, but in this circumstance they allowed a nurse to attend with Samantha. Even though the nurse was not formally invited by Julius as a possible wish recipient.

"Are you ready?" Robin asked Samantha after Dani was done. "You look stunning."

"Yeah?" Samantha answered in her coarse voice.

Robin administered the specific dose of pain medication the doctor called for and they both assisted Samantha carefully into the wheelchair. Samantha was dressed in a deep purple, cashmere robe, and white slippers. She had a glowing radiance that emitted through her smile, not from the accents applied by her friend, but from the hope that waited for her.

Robin slightly reclined the chair's backrest because of Samantha's weakness in her neck. She pushed her out of her room and into the hallway. Dani and Dominic remained in the room. They shared in the excitement for the possibility of her being selected from the group of invitees. They both stood at the doorway and watched as Samantha was ushered through the very halls that contained torment, despair, and hardship represented by patients fighting the adversity of illness. A patient in her final hours was now moving past rooms on either side, on

170

her way to join an event that would change someone's life forever. The intense pain that inflicted her earlier was now dulled by the medication, but her illness now caused slight tremors in her arms.

They turned and entered through a set of doors on the other side of the building. Once they were through, they ventured down a long, dimly lit corridor. Light gray walls and tan floors were as dull as could be, but the anticipation of what waited ahead added sparkle to the moment. One more turn and they approached a closed door that led to a private room. It was the conference area. Robin stopped just short of the entrance and walked around the wheelchair to open the door with a key she had. The door was propped open and Samantha felt the fluttering of butterflies in her stomach. Before entering, Mr. Harshom met them at the doorway from inside the room.

"Hello, Samantha," said the elder. "It's wonderful to see you here with us. You've been cordially invited to join in the thirty-third birthday celebration of Julius Christoff. Please come in."

"Thank you," Samantha replied and smiled.

As Robin glided Samantha through the doorway, they could see a remarkable setting before them. The room was transformed from an ordinary conference room into a more intimate atmosphere, unlike the boring room meant for business meetings. Samantha's eyes were set at ease from the lower light levels and warm color temperatures. The ceiling lighting was mostly dimmed to allow for the huge assortment of candles placed on both sides along the walkway in the center of the room. This led to a beautiful display of three pearl-white, tall candle holders that surrounded the main table. There stood Julius waiting patiently for his guests to arrive.

Robin began to slowly escort Samantha in her wheelchair down the candle-lit path. As they neared Julius, Samantha noticed the ceremonial elements on the table beside him. Mr. Harshom followed behind their procession patiently. Once they reached the main gathering area by the table, a wave of nervousness and excitement rushed over her pale demeanor. Samantha glanced around the gathering area and noticed enough space that could easily have dozens of people there. But, it was only Julius who stood patiently waiting for her. *Where were the other guests?* Perhaps she was the first to arrive.

Her hands continued to tremble and the onset of chills flooded her body. If it weren't for the pain medication she would feel internal misery from organ downfall. Robin positioned her wheelchair to one side and faced Samantha towards Julius and the elements. The nurse stood behind the chair to render any help Samantha may have required. Samantha looked around at the amazing display before her. She sat in awe at the grand scale of this event.

She looked at Julius and smiled.

"Happy birthday, Julius. Sorry, I don't have a gift," she said.

Her voice was not recognizable to Julius because of the extreme coarseness in her throat.

"Hello Samantha," Julius said as he approached her, leaned down, and then embraced her. "I'm so glad to see you."

His expression of concern for her was like no other and his voice projected a glowing enthusiasm.

"Welcome to my celebration of life. Don't worry about a gift. You've given me so much more than you can imagine."

He stood upright and thanked Robin for her assistance. He turned around and walked a few steps to where Mr. Harshom now stood next to the table of elements. He stopped and turned around to face her. Julius wore a white dress shirt, slacks, and leather dress shoes. His tall frame and confidence seemed to suggest he held a position of royalty or great importance.

Samantha was used to seeing him wearing more casual attire during their CU service. It was apparent to her that he highly valued this moment. But, now she wondered who Julius was beneath his kindness and meek character. He was more mysterious than before.

"Where are the others?" she asked.

"There are no others. I only invited you," Julius said as he grinned.

"What?" she replied with a look of shock. "Really?"

Those words struck her ailing and weakened heart. In her worst calamity, she felt a surge of pure hope penetrate her. She began to cry out of exhaustion and out of elation. This was a gesture of pure intention on behalf of Julius and he was about to offer her something that would rescue her.

Samantha was shocked and she raised her hands over her face. Her shoulders began to convulse and Robin consoled her. She knew the mighty weight of this moment and what this meant for her and Dominic. It meant life was about to shift from one to another; life from Julius to Samantha.

But, suddenly her thoughts shifted to how grave her condition was. Maybe she was too far gone to come out of the clutches of Stillwhorm. Perhaps it was just too late. Or maybe this would not be enough to bring her back from looming death.

Julius waved for her to come closer. His invitation was the beginning of her future.

"Come closer, please," he said.

Robin pushed Samantha toward Julius and stopped at the table. Once she was in place, the nurse stepped back several feet from them and observed from a distance.

Samantha wiped her tears and looked up at Julius. His kind face glowed from the radiance of the bright surroundings. Or, was it from his mere presence that was radiant from the perfect love he had for her. The love that one has in an act to freely give his life for another.

Mr. Harshom began his speech.

"All in attendance. You are witnesses to Julius Christoff's thirty-third birthday and his act of granting a wish transfer today. As an official member of the Council of Elders, I have been appointed to officiate Julius' birthday event."

Samantha couldn't believe this was happening. Mr. Harshom continued.

"Esid Arapym stands upon a pillar of the community. Immovable and strengthened by those who live within its vast borders. You both understand the importance of this appointment. Especially you, Samantha. And Julius has chosen the most powerful act anyone could participate in. His actions will soon demonstrate to the Council and this community what it means to sacrifice."

Mr. Harshom reached down to the stone-like flask set in front of him and began to carefully remove the seal. He turned to Julius.

"Julius Christoff. Would you please take your place at my side?"

With eagerness, Julius stepped closer to the elder. There was no hesitation or apprehension within him. He stood at his side and faced Samantha. Then, in that same monotone voice reserved only for this ceremony, Mr. Harshom began to speak slowly.

"Julius, you have answered the call. From your heart so deep within, you embrace a moment meant for those who wish for something sacred. Sacred for two lives: yours and another of your choice."

He stared directly into his face, into his waiting eyes.

"Julius, who have you selected to be the recipient of your sacred wish transfer?"

It was obvious that there was only one person who was present, unlike other ceremonies. But the formal traditions were to be adhered to, so the question must be asked. Samantha was in awe of the moment knowing full well she was to be rescued from her looming death. And she hoped it wasn't too late.

Without hesitation, Julius turned to her and answered Mr. Harshom.

"Samantha Parsons will be the recipient of my wish transfer."

The finality of his words melted Samantha's tortured heart. In her suffering, she sensed a powerful peace.

The Elder smiled with a sense of melancholy in his eyes as he stretched out and offered his hand to Julius. He knew what was at stake for Julius and he offered one last gesture of gratitude. Julius accepted and they shook hands.

Mr. Harshom then carefully removed the seal to the special flask. With both hands, he slowly lifted it to his face and he took in a deep breath then inhaled the aroma now emitting from the container. He was captivated with the sweet notes of the sacred nectar, almost as if he had never smelled this before. Then he lowered the container towards the chalice and began to pour. When the chalice was filled halfway to the gold brim he stopped and placed the flask back on the table. He paused slightly to reflect on the depth of this moment.

The elder took the chalice and looked at both Julius and Samantha.

"Now you must consider the agreement you have made and honor it, Julius. This is your moment."

Mr. Harshom turned and offered him the nectar. Julius gladly accepted it and looked at Samantha. Julius' gaze spoke volumes and was undeniably deliberate. His calm eyes offered her hope at this moment. Then he spoke and his words expressed precisely what she had expected to receive.

"This day is meant for you, Samantha. You have given your life for your son and, during your time of crisis, you still decided to offer others kindness and love. I have appointed you as my wish recipient long before your illness began to consume you. You were the one in my heart that I desired to offer this blessing to."

Her tears flowed profusely. Julius continued.

"Receive this gift freely and you will live with your son without any threat of illness for as long as you both live. This day and this moment are for you."

Julius placed the rim of the chalice to his lips and sipped a portion of the nectar. The sourness pricked his stomach as it flowed deep inside of him. It was like bitter wrath that invaded his pureness. The liquid seeped into his digestive system and began an assault on his organs and tissues. In a matter of seconds, he felt the decline of his health, from his inner core traveling out into each limb. Chaos overcame his senses. His tragedy began.

"You may now offer it to Samantha," instructed Mr. Harshom.

He graciously extended the chalice close to her reach as she sat in the wheelchair. She held up both of her frail hands, still trembling, and took hold of the chalice. She remembered the taste from her birthday celebration and knew the bitter nectar was foul. But she immediately brought it to her mouth and sipped new life.

Tingling began in her head and spread down into her shoulders. Then the sensation spread into her arms, through her chest, and out to her legs. Her shaky hands faded to stillness and the pain throughout her body ceased. Samantha had the sudden urge to stand. Without supporting the weight of her once nearly lifeless body, she confidently stood to her feet with new strength. She felt power in her tissues and vigor in every aspect of her being. Her strength had immediately returned and a new life was born where, just moments earlier, death had its clutches firmly upon her. She began to weep with a complete joyful expression.

Relieved, Mr. Harshom approached her with approval on his face, satisfied with the outcome and he took the chalice from her.

"Very good. I'm so very pleased," he said. "Congratulations."

Before she could reply, she noticed Julius struggle to remain standing as he began to sway. He held his head and closed his eyes from the pounding that raged from within. His arms trembled and the burning in his circulatory system felt like flaming poison. The nectar was striking his health with unrelenting punishment just as quickly as it was providing Samantha with restoration. He suddenly collapsed to the ground, lifeless and still.

"Julius!" Samantha shouted as they all rushed to his side.

He was gone. Life had escaped his flesh, bones, and tissues. The smiles that once portrayed a loving, sweet man had now been exchanged for a blank expression reserved for the deceased. It was no longer Julius who laid there, but a mere shell of his pleasant existence.

He died just minutes after he sipped the nectar and the wish transfer was completed. His passionate life could not elude his death sentence. It was his willful act of sacrifice that propelled him to such a fate. Even though his previous days were spent contemplating his decision with great agony, it was the joy of knowing Samantha was going to live again that ultimately persuaded him.

The horror of this scenario punched her in her gut with blunt force trauma. Samantha exchanged her joy for grief in an instant. She held his face and desperately wanted to say so much to him.

Robin attempted to perform resuscitation methods, but Mr. Harshom urged her to cease and gently held her arm to halt her efforts. There was nothing that could help him. The transfer had already been validated by the powerful agent.

As Samantha and the elder kneeled at his side, she turned to Mr. Harshom with outpouring tears and heartache.

"What happened to him?"

"I'm terribly sorry, Samantha. Julius had taken a severely potent formula of the nectar."

He paused for a moment, then he revealed to her the plan Julius had devised. His eyes were convincing as he looked directly into her brokenness.

"He came to my office recently one evening and asked if there was any way he could bring you back from calamity. Because your battle with Stillwhorm Syndrome had escalated into the final phase, it was nearly impossible. You required a much stronger antidote in your grave state of health. I warned him that by drinking this, the possibility of it causing a fatal blow immediately was likely. I warned him sternly."

Mr. Harshom then turned back to his lifeless body. He continued.

"But the adoration he had for you was more than the absolute death sentence he had to face. It was evident to me that his love for you and Dominic exceeded any obstacle that would interfere with his calling."

Samantha looked intently at the elder as he described the situation. It was nothing short of the beautiful love that was demonstrated by a willing man dedicated to bringing her back to life in this manner. The beauty of this love bathed her like a towering waterfall and rescued Samantha from the shackles of certain doom. She was awestruck and speechless at Julius's bold intention. He wanted to save her and nothing else mattered.

They all remained by his side for a while in honor of his commitment. No words were said. It was the mild sobbing that permeated the still air. Somehow, the grand decorations that surrounded them, were no longer appropriate. The celebration faded into sorrow for their friend. It seemed as though the conference room's brightness was dimming slowly.

Samantha would miss him dearly. It was another loss she had to endure. One more blow to her fragile heart.

CHAPTER 14

The next morning, Dr. Brimmer walked briskly from the cafeteria holding his fresh cup of coffee with one hand and a briefcase in the other. He took short sips carefully along the quiet hallways and already began thinking about the day ahead. His patients were on his mind before he ever entered the unit.

"Good morning, doctor," said the charge nurse cheerfully.

"Morning, Sherry," he replied.

"We have a big day ahead. Rounds by eight-thirty?" Sherry asked.

He flipped through the charts stacked on the desk. His eyes scanned through the evening's notes as he continued to sip on his morning cup of clarity. They were volumes of patient data with most cases of Stillwhorm. He frowned as he read some of the notes left by the night shift team. His mind focused on the details of each patient and he became surprised by what he learned.

"Doctor? Eight-thirty?" she asked again.

He caught himself from his momentary trance and looked up at her with a blank stare.

"Sorry. Uh, yeah. That's fine," he said.

His attention immediately shifted back to the charts. He flipped pages almost frantically as if he was on the brink of some terrific medical discovery. He was amazed.

"Sherry. Did you notice anything odd from the night shift briefings during this morning's shift change?"

He asked. Before she could answer, he continued to speak.

"I can't believe some of these overnight numbers. They're remarkable."

"Yeah. I'm surprised," she answered with a smile.

It was remarkable indeed. Every patient hospitalized for Stillwhorm Syndrome experienced significant improvement overnight. It wasn't merely a few of them or a large percentage, but it was each patient on the floor.

Their breathing rate had improved, oxygen levels stabilized, heart rate normalized—everything about their state of health seemed to dramatically shift in their favor, or at least that's how it looked on the surface.

Dr. Brimmer called the morning staff to the nurse's station for an urgent meeting. One by one, they assembled around the doctor.

"Are we all here? Yes? Good. So, I reviewed the charts from last night and I'm alarmed at the incredible shift of each patient's status. I mean this is incredible," he said with alarmed eyes.

His enthusiasm reverberated through the staff. They also sensed something very important had taken place since they had their meeting with the night shift nurses. But to see him bubble with a vibrancy this morning added to their curiosity.

"Please make quick rounds with your patients once we break and grab a blood sample so we can run that stat. As you do that, I'll meet with each one for a brief assessment."

"What is it?" asked Annie, one of the nurses.

"I think we are experiencing a wave of reversal across the board—Stillwhorm Syndrome may be ceasing in our patients. Something wonderful may have taken place," he said as he smiled, but held back some of his giddiness. "Let's go."

And with the purpose of a professional football team that suddenly breaks from a strategic huddle, the team scattered in all directions. They had their orders from their captain and shared in his exciting curiosity.

Dr. Brimmer washed his hands as he entered the first room. It was Phyllis Draper—a 58-year-old patient stricken with Stillwhorm three weeks prior. He greeted her as he walked to the sink and washed his hands. After he dried his hands quickly he approached her bed. She couldn't help but speaking before he could.

"Doctor. Good morning. I just want to say that I'm feeling so much better this morning. Whatever you did overnight sure did work."

"Hi, Phyllis. It's good to see you in good spirits today. How are you feeling?" he asked.

"Super! Strong! Like I said, whatever you prescribed last night worked very well."

Phyllis reached up to the ceiling with both arms to show him her newfound energy. Her grin was very convincing.

He chuckled and leaned over her bed as he positioned his stethoscope over his ears. He paused as she leaned forward in an upright position, eager to cooperate. His hand placed the other end on her back over her gown.

"Deep breath, please. Again. One more," he said.

He stood back up and was puzzled. His thoughts filtered through many ideas and possible scenarios, but his eyes gave his process away.

"Sound good?" said Phyllis.

"Uh, yeah. It's amazing. Why, just yesterday before I left, your lungs sounded like an asthmatic running a marathon. And this morning, they sound like brand new lungs. The disease attacked your lungs right from the get-go."

He wasn't sure what to say next.

"So, your nurse will be in to take a blood sample for testing. Okay?" he said as he turned to squirt a dollop of hand sanitizer onto his palm that was mounted to the wall by the door. "I'll be back later to check on you."

He walked out of her room and closed her door behind him. Then he made his way without haste to the next patient's room. He knocked and slowly opened the door.

"Henry? You awake?" he asked.

Henry Whitman, a 30-year-old patient who was fighting the disease for over two months now without any improvement. Up until this morning, he had been in-patient now for the last six days with weakness and fever. Today, he was sitting in a chair reading a book someone had given him weeks ago, but he did not have the desire to dive into it until now.

"Oh, hello doctor," he said. "Can I go home today?"

Dr. Brimmer chuckled nervously as he walked to the sink.

"Well, let's see how your blood work comes back this morning. Do you feel like you have a fever?" the doctor asked.

"Don't think so."

He washed his hands at the sink near the entrance and pulled a couple of paper towels from the dispenser. He dried his hands as he approached his patient.

"May I feel your head?" Dr. Brimmer asked.

"Sure," Henry replied.

The doctor felt Henry's head and the back of his neck.

"Hmmm. You were burning up last night. You feel fine right now."

"I know. I'd like to go home today," said Henry.

"Probably. Let me get back to you," said the doctor as he left the room.

The charge nurse met Doctor Brimmer in the hallway and interrupted his task of checking in on the patients. She looked puzzled.

"Doctor? All of our Stillwhorm patients are experiencing a completely different state of health today for some reason. I mean ALL of them! Can you tell me what is going on?" she asked.

"I can't say for certain," said Dr. Brimmer as he slowly shook his head in disbelief. "Something happened since I left the floor last night. Something tremendous and, dare I say, miraculous. I made no changes in treatment protocols before I went home and there's nothing I can honestly point to that would explain this. I really would like to see everyone's blood work results as soon as I can."

"Results will be back soon," she replied.

She turned and resumed collecting the samples taken from the nurses. Only a few more were needed and she would walk them all to the lab herself once they were turned in at the desk.

"Good morning Jim. How are you today?" asked Dr. Brimmer while he visited his next patient.

Jim was their most recent admission and he was in his first phase of the disease. A 23-year-old who felt the effects of Stillwhorm only two days prior.

"I feel great, doctor. I expected to be stuck here for a while but now I'm doing a whole lot better," said the patient.

"Let's check your vitals?" said the doctor.

After several minutes, he found no reason to think Jim was required to be inpatient for care. Dr. Brimmer was dumbfounded by this turn of events. It was remarkable.

"Let me see what your labs show, but I think you should be discharged today."

Dr. Brimmer continued meeting with every Stillwhorm patient on the floor as he waited for the results to return from the lab. His findings were consistent—every patient, regardless of age or length of treatment, experienced a tremendous turnaround. By leaps and bounds, they all felt as though their strength and energy were regained.

Within the hour, the doctor had met briefly with each patient. He was pleasantly surprised by this incredible anomaly. He wanted to be the first to declare that no one would ever be stricken with Stillwhorm Syndrome. Yes, if that were to ever happen he would be the happiest man in the land.

"Doctor, we have the results back," said the charge nurse as she entered the station.

"Finally. I've been on pins and needles for the last forty-five minutes," said the doctor.

She handed him a small stack of paperwork; they were each patient's results and he sifted through them with intense curiosity. His piercing eyes scanned details and his mind collected the data with a sharp focus. He turned to the next page and repeated his analysis. One by one, he realized there were consistencies in the blood of each patient. Striking changes that were unexplainable, yet proven by levels of specific proteins, white blood cell counts, and other factual data represented with these findings. He smiled as he turned to the charge nurse.

"This is amazing! They're all experiencing healing and in ways that can't be explained. Terrific!" His enthusiasm was heard across the hallway.

Other nurses began to assemble at the desk as they all were just as pleasantly surprised as the doctor was by everyone's change in health status. He broke down the details from the results for them. He used biological terms and physiological explanations they could understand. Yes, this was truly an amazing morning for the treatment center. It was a momentous occasion that required the faith of acceptance and not relies on stumbling through possible explanations. No, simply believe and walk through the moment just as it was.

"Well. Let's begin discharging procedures," said Dr. Brimmer to everyone as he held both fists in the air as if he just scored the game-winning home run.

~

Later that same morning across town, terrific joy arrived at the Parsons residence. It was in the form of perfect healing and the assurance of sensational hope. Although, the bitterness of their loss was a harsh reality. But at the same time, Julius would have wanted them all to experience heartfelt jubilee.

Dominic danced around their garden in a joyful celebration of his mother's victory. She joined in his parade and followed him around waving her hands in the air. It was a perfect day for them. The family had been sealed by two wish transfers. Nothing like the evil of Stillwhorm Syndrome, other illness or disease would ever inflict its harm upon them. No sickness would separate Samantha and Dominic during their lifetimes. They were immune.

Dani laughed at them as she walked out through the patio door and out to the garden. She wanted to join the jubilation.

"Hey, you two. I want in," Dani said as she jumped in line behind Samantha and added to the cheerfulness.

They laughed and skipped through the garden like giddy kids on the playground. Their elation was unmatched. Samantha was alive and well. Her health returned to a point where she felt younger and had more vitality than before her bout with the illness. The moment was as sweet as anything she ever felt before.

Then, a doorbell rang from inside the house. At first, they ignored the sound. A second ring caused Samantha to stop and answer the door. She walked into the house and through the kitchen towards the knocking. *Who could it be?* She thought. When she opened the door she saw Mr. Harshom standing there holding something.

"Good day, Samantha." It was the elder.

"Hello," she replied.

"I don't mean to interrupt, but I have this for you."

He lifted a unique box just like the one he held months earlier after she made her wish to transfer. Samantha gratefully accepted the item. She knew precisely what it was.

"Thank you. Would you like to come in?"

"I appreciate your offer. But no thank you," he said. "I have some things I must attend to and I should leave. Have a wonderful day with your son," he said then he turned to walk away.

"Mr. Harshom?" she said. He paused and turned to look at her. "Will, I ever see you again?"

He smiled and answered.

"I think you already know the answer to that question, Samantha. You and Dominic now have a deep connection with Mara and with the Council of Elders. I'm sure I will be seeing you at the appropriate time."

He continued walking towards his car parked in front of her home.

She stood there puzzled and wondered what he meant. She looked down at the deep, crimson red box. It had the name: JULIUS CHRISTOFF in pearly white letters painted on the surface and the number "33" was in the lower right-hand corner. She didn't bother to open it. She knew a dignified dead crow was placed inside. And she was right. A special crow had died as part of the wish transfer Julius had made. It was Jasper assigned to the ceremonial death in exchange for life.

Samantha began to realize this crow was also Dominic's guardian. The one who protected him and watched over him. The crow he saw at his window and outside in their yard. The one Dominic colored in his book and carried around with him. Somehow, Samantha distinctly knew this was the crow that meant so much to her son and she couldn't tell him it was now dead. So, she took the box and hid it in her room until it was time to bury it.

She returned to the laughter outside. Dani and Dominic did not cease to play out their joyful antics.

"Who was at the door?" asked Dani.

"Oh, just a neighbor," Samantha replied.

"Sam, come and join us!" said Dani as she and Dominic ran in large circles while holding hands.

His giggling and laughter set the tone of the party. Dominic had no more concern for losing his mother. Instead, he felt the secure embrace of the love that held them both. It was the love of a friend, Julius that made all of this possible. Dominic's future looked bright and his reality had now changed.

They spent the better part of the late afternoon parading themselves into the evening. They wore party hats and sang silly songs. Except for Russell's absence, they were a complete family. Dani was now cemented into their lives by the nature of traumatic events that had transpired. And Samantha loved her best friend dearly for her devotion during a bleak and desperate time.

Samantha's mind often waned into sadness about Julius. It was such a tragedy at a young age. But she also held him in such high regard for his gift of life. She knew he would want her to continue living to the complete fullness she had dreamed of. It would be her desire to further his work at Compassion United and honor his legacy for as long as she could.

~

The weather was as perfect as it usually was. The wild fragrance of innumerable poppies, daisies, and raging wildflowers delighted Samantha's senses. The bluest skies draped over their heads and reminded them that paradise was closer than they thought. They returned to their spot in the country the following day after she regained her life. They were able to find the previous spot they visited during the last outing. And it was a perfect day to bury the crow given to her by the elder.

"Mommy? Did you bring the shovel?"

Dominic asked as they unpacked their things from the car.

"We have everything we need for this wonderful day," she said.

"It's a perfect day."

His grin made the sound of his voice brighter.

"I like it here," he said.

"So do I," Dani chimed in.

They sat on an outstretched blanket and admired the grand beauty visible for miles in all directions. Dominic was alright with the burial they were there to perform. Samantha had a talk with him days before the trip and explained how much of an honor it is to lay it to rest. He understood that his guardian crow, Jasper, had the most significant purpose for their family. Not only a watcher over him but being the actual crow in a long line of chosen ones to represent wish transfer grantors in Esid Arapym was a tremendous honor among their own. Especially for its direct sacrifice for his mother's life.

At the beginning of wishes long ago there was the first one chosen, a crow named Zion who became the initial representative of Mara, the sacred fruit, and the first wish transfer. And from that point on and with each crow, lives were exchanged—ones who would sacrifice their own life for someone else they cared for dearly. Thus began the chronicles of the consecrated wish transfers and the legacy of the sacrificial crows.

"Dommie?" said Samantha. "Why don't you go on ahead of us and find the perfect spot for the burial. Dani and I will follow behind."

"Really?"

He answered with a spark of happiness.

"Wow. Thanks."

Samantha turned to Dani and handed her the shovel.

"Why not? Let's give him the choice."

"Yeah," said Dani.

She accepted the shovel and waited for Samantha who retrieved the special box from the trunk. Once she had it they turned and noticed Dominic had already started his journey.

Dominic hurried through open fields of tall grass; the untamed foliage and beautiful landscape awarded him with its stunning peace. Beneath the breathtaking splendor of the immense skies, stained with the deepest blues, he made his way through this part of paradise. Dani and Samantha walked behind his trail casually as they too enjoyed the scenic surroundings. It was healing and blissful. They talked about what life would look like in the future and how Samantha was so elated to live out her days with Dominic at her side.

As they admired the wonder, they saw Dominic up ahead of them making his way towards a magnificent area. It was Mara that stood proudly with its powerful, majestic awe. Almost as if it was inviting them to visit with open arms. Yes, he chose his favorite place, aside from his own home; he chose to bury his guardian friend at the foot of the magnificent tree.

He stopped directly beneath its coverings of dense leaves and reached out his hand to touch its trunk. He smiled and looked upward at how glorious it was. There were numerous crows perched among the countless thick branches and Chancellor watched down upon him from his post. Dominic felt safe there. He sensed a presence of unmatched strength that guarded him. He smiled graciously at all of them and spoke.

"Thank you for helping me and my mother," Dominic said to the tree and all of the crows.

Chancellor cawed loudly in agreement and flew down to the boy. It remained in flight as it hovered before Dominic. The boy was impressed with how majestic this crow was. He knew Chancellor possessed incredible strength and power.

Then Mara spoke to his mind.

"I am very pleased, Dominic. You are welcome."

He smiled back.

"Do you remember your dream about Clyde's attack and how he was defeated?" asked Mara. "If you recall, it was Jasper—crow Thirty-three, that ended his existence. And that is what unfolded in your mother's redemption. The other slain crows represented the previous ones that gave their lives in wish transfers over time. Jasper gave its life, as well as Julius, for this most powerful wish transfer yet. In the process, Clyde was also eradicated."

"Wow," said Dominic. His young mind understood most of what he was told. These layers of truths would be fully comprehended as he grew.

Samantha and Dani now reached the tree as well. They stood in amazement of Mara's mammoth size and the large group of crows assembled within it. Samantha also felt the security of being in that place, just as Dominic felt. It was unexplainable, but also undeniable.

"Dommie. You chose a perfect spot here," said Samantha.

Dominic stood confidently as he answered.

"I did."

Dominic walked to his mother and took the box from her. Chancellor continued to hover above them. He took his guardian's coffin and walked a few steps back from Mara's trunk. He glanced up at the tree and paused.

"Right here," he said.

Dominic turned around and faced Dani and his mother.

"Right here."

Dani approached his chosen area with the shovel in her hands. She began to dig and Samantha stood next to her and Dominic. With each plummet of the shovel into the grassy earth, a few crows began to fly down and encircle them all. By the time the hole was large enough for the box, there were at least a hundred crows that stood at attention on the ground. Chancellor was the last to land at the feet of Dominic. Dani stepped back to allow Dominic access to the grave. He walked to the unearthed ground holding the box and Chancellor walked by his side. The boy knelt with great respect and carefully set the coffin into the grave. He held his hand over the name and number, then touched the box with his right hand.

"Thank you, Julius."

His voice was solemn and oddly reverent coming from a young boy.

"Thank you, Jasper. I won't forget you."

He removed his hand from the top of the box and stood upright.

"Mommy, can you say something?" he asked.

"Sure," she said as she smiled at him.

Samantha walked next to Dominic and put her arm around him. She stared down at the top of the box with an intense look on her face. She studied the name and number that was painted on the surface for several seconds. They flooded her emotionally like a rushing wind swirling around an empty room. *Julius Christoff* and *Thirty-three* looped in her mind continuously. After a very long pause, she spoke with tears falling.

"Life is precious, life is sweet, and it is a wonder. But even the best of our years are filled with pain and heartache. Soon those years will disappear...and we fly away."

She wiped teardrops from her eyes and her cheeks. She looked down at her son who glanced up at her too with such adoration. Dani slowly walked over to them and embraced them from behind. After a long reverent pause, Dani stepped around them and began filling the hole with the shovel. There was a silence that could be felt by every single person and living thing. The box was now completely covered by the dirt and formed a large mound. She knelt down and gently but firmly patted the dirt.

When she stood up the sound began. Dozens upon dozens of ear-piercing caws from the mass grouping of crows erupted. The grand chorus pierced the stillness of the countryside and echoes of their shouts could be heard for long distances. Then immediately their shrieks ceased all at once. The quietness resumed and the collective strength in their number could be sensed. Then they all began to lift off the grass in flight like an arsenal of rockets blazing into the sky. They flew in a large circular pattern over Mara about a hundred yards up. It was a wonderful sight to behold; a squadron of crows that flew above them in a clockwise formation and of unprecedented numbers. Except for Chancellor—it continued to hover in front of Dominic with its mighty wings flapping effortlessly.

Without words, Dominic knew what this crow was doing. It somehow communicated to the boy and it reassured him that it would now become his guardian; a reassignment. He was now granted the ability to comprehend the thoughts of the crows and his words were understood by them as well. Mara granted the boy with this level of awareness.

Chancellor would resume where Jasper had ended its service to Dominic and a powerful bond between the two was formed. Another crow would rise to be the leader and sole protector of Mara.

Suddenly, a crow returned from the parade in the sky and swooped down to Chancellor. They both hovered, faced each other, and Chancellor began to caw as if it was giving orders to the next in command.

Dominic stood in awe of the portrayal of allegiance to their calling and of their devotion to Mara. It was a moving sight to behold.

When Chancellor was done speaking, the other crow let out a unique single shout—the sound was similar to a high-pitch roar that brought chills to those standing there—and they both touched beaks. Then, as two swords striking each other, they quickly scraped their iron-like beaks together causing a flash of sparks. The other crow flew up to Mara to take its newly assigned position: commander of the crows and the tree's chief guard in service with perfect allegiance.

Dominic, Samantha, and Dani were amazed. They looked up to the tree and the crow was now at its post within the crow's den, at its place of commitment and command. The crow had a bright red glow in its eyes, making it distinguishable from the others, and it let out another lengthy shout as if it announced its presence. As its beak was open, thick, reddish-orange steam was exhaled.

Then Dominic looked over at Chancellor who still hovered beside him.

"I know its name," he said to Chancellor as Dominic pointed to the crow now perched in the tree. "That crow is Michael."

He turned to his mother and confirmed with a grin.

"This is Michael who now leads the crows and protects Mara. And Chancellor will be my guardian."

Samantha nodded. She also understood the unspoken reality of these mysterious truths concerning Mara and the crows. They now both possessed revelation and insight into these new things. Dominic experienced visions and dreams since he could remember. They were foretold about this time with Mara and with the crows. Yes, the tree began luring the boy since he was younger. It wasn't until Samantha willed her decision to drink from the cup of sacrifice that Mara began revealing to her and open her mind to the tree's reality. Samantha's and Dominic's enlightenment would be a significant strength within their family.

The boy stood with courage and with confidence among the crows and Mara. His vision was cemented by a bond forged by a painful sacrifice from his mother and her friend, Julius. The Parsons family held a unique insight granted only by those willing to lay down their own life for another. And for Samantha, she was gifted with the blessing of residing on both ends of this mysterious dichotomy. Her path was now diverted into a brand new future surrounded by all that is spectacular.

CHAPTER 15

The light of a brand new day peered through the edges of her bedroom drapes. It gently kissed her on the forehead and Samantha felt its warmth within her sleep. She leisurely opened her eyes and stared at the sliver of new sunlight. It caught her attention and called her by name with enticement. She remained in that moment for a long while.

Sleep was now serene. Her dreams were filled with lofty and playful excursions; no longer being stricken with toxic and deadly scenes. Now she awakens from her rest and fully understands the depth of her existence. Life became more precious than it ever was before. Before her wish transfer.

One week had now passed since Julius gave his life for her. There were moments when she spent time alone in her garden thinking about how much she missed Russell and that it would have been wonderful if he had been the recipient of a wish transfer. Her love for him remained deep and constant. And other times her thoughts brought her to those memories with Julius, Frank, and Naomi. When they would spend hours upon hours delivering smiles and comfort to those in the medical center. Samantha had not seen Frank or Naomi since Julius's memorial service when they said their final farewells to their beloved friend and leader.

Samantha felt it was time for some personal care. She had recently decided to change her hairstyle and shorten it. The long bob suited her petite frame very well and even enhanced her already pretty features. Dani agreed with her decision and encouraged her best friend to do more things for herself.

You could say that the Parsons residence was steeped in perfect peace. Samantha had her son and Dominic had his mother. Together they rested in that place of serenity while moving forward into their future.

She walked over to her large window and pulled open the drapes to view the morning beauty outside. This new day would bring more brightness to her life and she was prepared for all of that wonder. She took in a deep breath as her eyes scanned the landscape in the distance, then exhaled in awe of her world. Finally, she was able to see a parallel between the marvel displayed in Esid Arapym and the days and the years ahead. The symmetry of them brought perfect harmony.

Her smile was evidence of her state of peace. She could now dance in her heart and leap for the highest heights in her dreams. Samantha was eternally grateful.

Her eyes glanced at the clock. Eight twenty-five was an unusually late start for her, but she often stayed up into late evening hours reading and sipping on her tea. There were no schedules to keep lately because Dominic had a break from school. She went to take a shower after she glanced in on Dominic who was already playing with his toys in his room.

As the morning unfolded over breakfast and with the funny banter between her and Dominic, he asked to be excused from the table to play outside in the garden. He set his plate and cup in the sink and darted out the door. Samantha sat at the table and glanced at him periodically through the window.

The telephone interrupted the calm of the new day and Samantha answered the incoming call.

"Hello?" she said.

"Good morning, Samantha."

A man said on the other end.

"Oh, Dr. Brimmer. It's so good to hear from you," she replied.

"I hope I didn't wake you, but I had to call and see how you've been," he said. "The nurses ask about you all the time."

Samantha's grin could be felt through her words.

"You know, I'm doing extremely well. I can't tell you how many times I jump for joy almost literally. I'm so happy how everything has turned out for us."

He couldn't resist smiling. He was so elated for her, considering where she had once been. Dangling from a string above her absolute death just before her wish recipient moment.

"I am so very happy for you and Dominic. Tell me, how is our champion doing?"

"He's great. Playing and learning at school. He's fascinated with everything that has taken place since my recovery. Especially with the crows," she explained.

"Crows?" I don't understand," said the doctor.

"Well, he's fond of these crows from a specific part of the country we visit," said Samantha. "I can't explain it, but I think they have a special bond with him."

"Oh. Well, then that's just terrific," he said still a bit confused. "I'd like to see you both. Maybe you could come by the center soon. You know, Robin is always thinking about you. She just can't wrap her head around how sick you were and now how this whole experience has brought you a new life."

"Well, we'd like that. Maybe later this week," she said.

"Great. Can hardly wait," he replied. "Oh, by the way, have you heard about how things have been around here?"

"No. What's going on?" Samantha asked.

"Ever since that day you made your full recovery with your wish transfer, we haven't seen any new patients. You know, with

Stillwhorm Syndrome," he said. "Not one new case has come through our doors and we're all baffled. Even our existing patients suddenly became well. We discharged all of them. I mean we're delighted, of course, but baffled."

"Are you kidding me?" Samantha was so surprised. "That's wonderful. Is there anything you can attribute this to?"

"No. No idea whatsoever. But we'll gladly take it. I don't like treating people with that disgusting disease," he said with disdain. "It used to destroy lives. Not today."

"I'm happy to hear. I hope it continues," she said.

"Listen, take care and we'll be seeing you later this week. Bye, Samantha."

"Thank you for calling, doctor," she said then hung up the phone.

She stared off into space for a few moments as she tried to understand this strange phenomenon. As wonderful as it was, she couldn't shake the curiosity behind it. *Was Esid Arapym finally rid of this horrible disease? And if so, how did this happen? Why does it seem to coincide with my healing?* These were some of the thoughts that raced through her mind. Regardless of how and why it was a victory nonetheless for the community and for all who hope for long life with family and friends.

What she did not know, but soon would come to the realization, is that Julius made a tremendous sacrifice. And not only for her but for every person living in Esid Arapym. He held a unique position, a calling. A purpose dedicated to bringing healing to the land. Without public knowledge, he held onto this mission privately. Yet, he knew the extreme power held within his life.

Through many years spent with Mara, Julius was shown these insights since his youth, and his journey to bring healing to the land was revealed to him over a great period. His father introduced him to Mara when he was a child and that is when purpose began to pour into him. The child ultimately grew into a man and his eyes were keenly set upon a perfect commission. And he appreciated every moment spent under Mara's powerful shadow. Yes, he highly regarded his visits with the tree throughout his life.

Mara spoke truth into Julius and that became a powerful force within him. His intense care and love for others were cultivated and ripened from a tree's unending devotion. His character was shaped and hope was formed through him. Every day he spent pouring into others was one more day nearer to the close of his ministry. That one day was chosen for him to release a miracle upon the land and for his dear friend Samantha—on his thirty-third birthday.

Samantha's attention was distracted by the laughter that erupted outside from Dominic. She walked over to the door and glanced out of the window to see what he was doing. Her eyes couldn't believe the scene. Samantha stepped forward as she opened the door to take a closer look.

There in her spacious backyard was a group of crows; seven that huddled on the grass around Dominic. Of course, Chancellor was there and she perceived a conversation between them both occurring. Dominic would pause as if he was listening then he would giggle and answer with his words. Speaking with the crows was a common occurrence now.

"I'm ready!"

He shouted and, within a flash of movement, the group of birds leaped on him almost as a predator pounces its prey. Then, in a smooth maneuver, the group of crows led by Chancellor swiftly flapped their wings with each one grasping a part of the boy's clothing. They carried him upwards into the sky effortlessly. Dominic let out a loud howl as he was taken upward into the air. He was eager and thrilled to be taken up into the sky just as the crows did for his mother. They referred to it as "crow flight."

Samantha ran towards them in a rush of adrenaline and pure excitement; she did not feel he was in any danger and trusted them fully. She stopped and cheered for him as they carried him up into the sky and as they circled above the tree line at the edge of her vast garden. It looked like a victory lap for a successful training day. But, it was merely another level of awakening Dominic had with Chancellor, the crows, and Mara. He laughed and chuckled as he was lifted over the tops of trees and eventually out of her sight.

Samantha chuckled to herself and, in pure amazement at what she witnessed, she began to clap her hands in applause. She recollected how the crows carried her out of the dark woods in their rescue operation. Suddenly she could hear many distant cries echo across the sky as if thunderclaps pounded the atmosphere. They were caws chanting in massive concert from a distance; their resounding victory chants announced a new awakening in Dominic. It was impressive. This was his first test flight with them. The first of many more flights to come.

Suddenly, a well of deep emotion sprung up from within and she began to speak as she stared up into the sky.

"Fly, Dominic, fly. Soar across the burnt orange horizon lit with the flames of the bright morning sun. Crow flight will carry you there. To the place where you belong and where your dreams will become a new reality. Over the plains and above the clouds. This is your playground and your dimension to inhabit."

He was now an heir to the inheritance that was enacted by Solomon Childs long ago. A generational passage of power through life-giving wish transfers. Dominic was now an important vessel among the dominion of Mara. And the crows knew his name—they served vigilantly alongside his thriving and raging spirit.

Mara gave charge over them as Dominic willed. He would forge through his destiny with zeal and conviction. Together with Chancellor, they were an alliance that will make the darkness tremble. And they were ready to protect Esid Arapym from any threat that opposed the unprecedented tranquility that fell upon this land.

With one act from an agent of selfless love, the once ailing people of this land were now released from the agony of death from the agent of disease and preserved by Julius and his calling. Where all who reside within its borders call it their paradise. And to Samantha, it had now become a place of perfect peace. Where Stillwhorm Syndrome was eradicated from her life and banished from her years ahead—tomorrow and every day after. Where her heart continued to heal from the tremendous loss of Russell, but she forged through such valleys with her son at her side. Her future was promised with a brighter hope.

Samantha discovered realized sanctuary. A fresh beginning in a place of refuge. She was secure and treasured this newfound future. She looked ahead with confidence and reassured her son that their lives would be kept under the watch of Mara.

The legacy of the crows lived on within the hearts and the minds of the few who knew the mystery of Mara. Their sacrifices in connection with the rare wish transfers were honored. Crows—once considered ordinary birds by some—were held in much higher regard for their role in history, their dedication to safeguarding lives, and their amazing power.

The passage of truth behind the legacy would follow down the trail to the next generation. What commenced as a single act of sacrifice by Zion, the first crow to offer itself long ago, unraveled into a collection of magnificent deeds of surrender for something greater than themselves. Samantha was graced by the dedication of her appointed crow for Dominic's preservation, followed by Jasper for Julius and his gift for Samantha. One by one, they fell willingly. In all, they numbered *thirty-three crows*.

~

One blissful morning, she sat quietly and gazed out of her window while holding Dominic tightly in her arms. Samantha rested simply in awe of what they now securely possessed. Waves of calm and joy comforted her previous battle-weary heart. In a faint exhale she whispered as she kissed him on his forehead–

"My paradise."

Esid Arapym.

THE END

Life is precious, life is sweet, and it is a wonder. But even the best of our years are filled with pain and heartache. Soon those years will disappear…and we fly away.

AUTHOR BIO

Roger R. Ziegler is a youth leader in his community and enjoys storytelling. He is married to the love of his life and they have raised four wonderful children. Through the adversity in life, he has learned to draw from these years that have shaped him and sends hope to those who may be hurting.

Roger R. Ziegler

In his third book, his first novel, he explores a land of fiction and dives into a world created from personal experiences. Thirty-three Crows is the first of three books. The next will be a prequel followed by a sequel to end the saga.

His previous books are available on Amazon:

Patchwork Kid: A Boy's Transplant Journey of Hope through the Midst of Tragedy explores the life of his son, Noah, who faced incredible odds as he fought a life-threatening illness.

The Hope Parade: Bringing Encouragement, Comfort, and Glorious Expectations Into Your Adversity shares the powerful hope Roger has known through the darkest moments in life.

Made in the USA
Las Vegas, NV
01 November 2021

33496000R00125